Cajun Heat

Charlene A. Berry

INDIGO

Indigo is an imprint of
Genesis Press, Inc.
315 Third Avenue North
Columbus, Mississippi 39701

Copyright © 1999 by Charlene A. Berry

Cajun Heat

ISBN 1-885478-59-3

Manufactured in the United States of America

FIRST EDITION

Cajun Heat

Dedication

To my family. Thanks for supporting me in everything.

To Queen, for her spiritual words of wisdom and love.

To Crystal, for showing me the true side of being a woman.

To Sylvia, thanks for being hard on me—really!

And last but not least, here's to Beautiful—and you know who you are. Many thanks.

Cajun Heat

If my people, who are called by my Name, will humble themselves and pray, seek my face and turn from their wicked ways, then I will hear from heaven and forgive their sin and will heal the land.

2 Chronicles 7:14

$\mathcal{O}ne$

Detective Symone Rawlins of the Baltimore City Police Department drove with her eyes deadlocked on the road in front of her. When most people were still asleep, Symone's day had already begun.

As the black Miata speedily cut through a lingering mist at 4:45 a.m., the round headlights of the sports car seemed to beam into infinity. The glass of the windshield reflected the iridescent light of the moon high above. It was the beginning of a not-so-perfect day.

Crazy thoughts plagued Symone's mind as she exceeded the 65 mph speed limit. Could she go through with it? What would she gain by being there? She wondered if she could ever forgive herself for losing Jordan, her dear sweet brother.

He had been so beautiful. Jordan had had a smile that could make the rain seem like sunshine. Even now, though her heart was heavy, Symone's memories of him were fond ones.

She had been so proud of him. At times when she was down, Jordan would always give her priceless pearls of wisdom. Symone's life had evolved around his.

But now he was gone. Taken away by an evil man so wretched that the mere thought of him knotted and nauseated her stomach.

A year had passed since Jordan's death and the pain was as real as if it all had happened yesterday. The only thing that had kept her going was the insuppressible fury of revenge that festered deep within her soul.

For a long time, she had blamed herself for Jordan's death. There wasn't a day that went by that she didn't relive the horror over and over again in her mind. Sometimes she could still hear the explosion ringing in her ears.

It had all begun with an anonymous phone call. Across town, a suspected burglar had tried to break into an abandoned machine shop. Since Symone and Jordan patrolled that area, it had only been natural for them to respond.

Jordan was fresh out of the academy and Symone thought it only right that she and her brother be partners. At first, Lieutenant Spaulding had refused to assign the two together, but since she was one of the best officers on the force, she knew he wouldn't refuse her. Plus, Symone wanted to be the one to break her "rookie" brother in instead of someone else.

As they approached the building in broad daylight, nothing seemed out of the ordinary. In fact, the old industrial area looked as it always did on a Sunday, abandoned and empty. As she slowed her vehicle and put on the emergency lights, Symone decided to check it out.

She parked the car and she and Jordan got out.

"I'll check around back. You check the front," she told him as she approached the side of the building.

With her weapon drawn, Symone proceeded with caution. It wasn't unusual for drug dealers to conduct business behind secluded areas like this one.

Alert and ready for anything, she peered through the grime-coated windows. The inside of the building was dim. Scattered boards, metal beams and a few ripped-out walls covered the floor. The only things moving were motes of dust particles floating in slow motion in a stray shaft of sunlight. But suddenly, out of nowhere, something or somebody darted across the room toward the back of the building.

Instantly, Symone went into pursuit mode. She felt the adrenaline in her body escalate. Her breathing became rapid as she raced along the side of the building. The sound of her feet pounding the ground, along with the jingling of her keys in her pocket, and the dangling handcuffs attached to her holster, seemed to take on a rhythm of their own.

Symone ran toward the back of the building, hoping to catch her suspect attempting to flee. That's when it happened.

A heart-stopping explosion that sounded like a rocket igniting. The blast was so intense that the force of the exploding walls flung Symone's body into a pile of metal beams and lumber. She figured the sound of the blast would trigger car alarms several blocks away.

A dark, massive cloud of smoke ascended toward the clear, cloudless sky. Burnt particles of flying debris and rubble seared and sizzled on the ground around her. Barely conscious and trapped under flaming plywood, hot bricks and other material, Symone moaned in agony. Pain assailed every part of her body as she regained her senses. Bits of broken rocks rolled away as she pushed her way clear from under parts of what had once been a brick building. Hurt, she reached for the mouthpiece of the walkie-talkie. Her hand was cut and bleeding. She spoke into the microphone: "Officer down. Officer down." She tasted blood on her lips.

As a breeze brushed over her, she experienced a cooling sensation on her head and face. She reached up and felt the wetness rolling down the side of her face. She touched her head, looked at her hand and saw blood. Open cuts seemed to be on her head, ears and mouth.

Symone struggled to get to her feet. She screamed in pain as her legs gave way to the pressure. She looked down and saw a large gash on her leg through a rip in her pants. But her health was the least of her worries.

"Jordan! Jordan!" she yelled.

With every ounce of strength she could muster, she finally got on her feet. Symone dragged her shattered body through burning rubble to find out if her brother was all right. She heard the sound of sirens in the distance. As she hobbled to what had been the front entrance to the building, she saw how bad the damage was.

"Jordan, answer me!" Bricks and wood had been thrown clear through the front windshield of the patrol car. She stood there, bowed over as tears streamed down her blood-stained face. Frantically she looked around until her eyes fell on what appeared to be a hand sticking out from beneath a crumbled wall, the front door of the shop on top of it.

She quickly limped over and fell down beside Jordan. With the strength of five men, she managed to lift the crumbled wall and smoking door off her brother's body.

"Jordan," she cried, lifting his head into her arms. His face was burned and badly cut. She wiped his face with her hand. Her blood and tears mixed with the black ash that had masked his face.

"C'mon. Open your eyes," she begged him. "I know you can hear me. Open your eyes." Jordan lay still, cradled in her arms like a baby. "Wake up, dammit! Jordan, please open your eyes." She wept, fearing the worst. Her heart exploded inside with indescribable sorrow. She was as empty as the skeleton building still burning behind her.

Jordan was dead and, as far she was concerned, so was she.

"Noooo!" With her face lifted toward a black sky, Symone cried out like a restless Bangui.

Symone shook her head free of the nightmare of that day her brother died, tried to concentrate on the road, forcing the painful memories to subside, but the tears in her eyes burned as she approached her exit.

"Damn you, Blade." For two whole years, she had cursed that name. But tonight, Kevin Stokes, alias Johnny Blade, was going to get what he deserved. The thought of finally getting even brought a bitter smile to her lips. The grimace replaced the sea of tears she brushed away with her hand.

With a sudden surge of assurance and anticipation, Symone jammed the car into high gear and floored the gas pedal. Choking the steering wheel as she sliced through the darkness, she took a hairpin turn onto her exit.

Fayette Street was glowing under the streetlights as she made her last lap off the beltway. The Maryland State Penitentiary was lit up like a Christmas tree.

As she slowly approached the guarded gate, she saw that mobs of people had gathered outside the barbed-wire fence to protest the execution. She stopped momentarily to read some of the signs that were held high in the air. She could clearly see who was for the execution and who was against it. One read: "An Eye For An Eye, Execute Him", while yet another read: "Only God Condemns". The two groups seemed to be having a standoff along the fence line. Tempers flared and angry words were exchanged between the two groups.

Symone sat in her car, dazed. All she knew was that she had suffered a great loss. A loss that could never be replaced. Then she wondered, will an execution be enough?

As she proceeded to make her way to the guarded security gate, a team of heavily armored officers marched past her car and into the crowd of protesters. They had been called in for crowd control, no doubt. They stomped in sync and formed a human wall between the groups of spectators to avoid further confrontation.

When she approached the guard at the gate, Symone flashed her badge to the security guard. He verified her authority and allowed her car to pass.

Symone pulled up in front of the prison and parked beside a row of police cruisers. She stepped from the car and gazed up at the sky. She saw how the sun was attempting to push its rays through the darkness. Finally, it appeared on the horizon. It was the first time she had ever seen the moon and the sun share such a vast space together. The sight of the two lights in the sky had an ominous look about it. Strangely, she considered the lucid powers of the two orbs to be the light and the dark sides of her life. It was as if the sun had risen to bring light to an endless darkness she had been in for too long.

Then, almost as if she was commanded, Symone squared her shoulders, took a deep breath, turned and began to walk toward the door that would finally close a sad chapter in her life.

As she stood at the door, a rotating camera caught her face. She knew her image was being transmitted onto a small monitor at a desk just inside the door. She was buzzed in, and as the door closed behind her, she could still hear the angry voices of the crowd.

At the desk, a correctional officer sat waiting. Symone stepped in and showed her badge. "Your weapon, detective," he said.

Symone pulled from the 9mm from her back holster. She disengaged the magazine, opened the slide, and handed them both to the officer.

"Sign in, please," he said.

She picked up the pen and signed her name to a long list of other officials who had come to witness the execution. As she scanned down the sheet, she noticed one name that surprised her, Mayor Collins. She had heard him say on the news the day before that he would not attend the execution.

Another officer led her down a short corridor to the observation room from which the execution would be viewed.

When they arrived, there was another armed guard at the door. The sign on the door read: Authorized Personnel Only. He unlocked the door and Symone stepped inside.

As soon as she placed her foot on the bare floor, an immense feeling overwhelmed her. Her body teetered against the door as her attention was drawn to the two-way mirror. On the other side was the execution chamber. Sitting in the middle of the room was a portentous electric chair. Symone's eyes locked onto it. Under the glare of a single light, the chair had an eeriness about it. Just the sight of it made the hair on her arms stand up.

The chair itself appeared cold and hard; the thick leather straps hung loose—waiting, anticipating its next victim. Symone's all-too-human side wouldn't allow her to harbor any remorse for a person who got pleasure out of murdering people, including her brother. But there was still that small voice inside her head that wanted her to forgive and forget.

No! she screamed inwardly. She had been waiting a long time for this moment, and now was no time for her to get soft.

Charlene A. Berry

She suddenly felt a light pressure around her arm. She turned and saw Omar, her new partner. She had expected him; she had seen his name on the sign-in sheet.

Symone immediately read his face. She knew that Omar had thought she wouldn't be there. But he was wrong.

"What are you doing here? You're suppose to be on administrative leave until further notice," he whispered in her ear. Symone acknowledged his presence but not his question. Not even Omar could have kept her from this moment. This day was what she had been waiting for.

"I could ask you the same question. But why play word games when we both know why we're here?" Symone's tone was sharp and abrupt. She hadn't meant to come off so hard on Omar. In fact, it had been he and his wife, Monica, who had opened their home to Symone after Jordan's death. They had grown fond of her and considered her family.

Omar didn't respond—at least not right away. He viewed her from the corner of his eye. "So we're here for the same reason—to see this bastard fry," he said at last.

Symone grunted, her eyes fixed on the chair in front of her. She processed mental pictures in her head as her eyes moved from one side of the execution chamber to the other. It almost felt as if she were checking the room, going over it inch by inch. There was no way of escape. The only way in was one door that had no knob, only a keyhole. And the only way out for that murderous monster was the electric chair.

Warden Louis Smiley and Lieutenant John Spaulding walked in. Spaulding was Symone and Omar's commander.

Symone and Omar turned and made eye contact with the lieutenant. Symone acknowledged her superior with a nod.

"I'll be back," Omar whispered to Symone, who remained unmoved by the presence of the warden and Spaulding.

Omar walked to the two men and, with a firm handshake, greeted the warden and his lieutenant, who pulled Omar to the side.

"Was bringing her here your idea?" The lieutenant's words were loud enough for Symone to hear.

Omar shook his head. "You know as well as I do that once her mind's made up, that's it—end of discussion."

His wrinkled brow, twisted bottom lip, and concerned look in his deep-set, dark eyes made Lt. Spaulding seem as if he had a lot on his mind. From where she stood, Symone could tell that Spaulding was worried about her.

It was now 5:45 a.m. The execution was scheduled to take place at six o'clock sharp. Almost simultaneously everyone standing had glanced down at their watches. Amongst the official members of the police force, there were a handful of civilians in attendance.

By special request of the judge, several of the victims' families had been invited to sit in on the execution. During his nine-month killing spree, Blade had murdered twelve people, two of whom had been high school students. And one police officer, Jordan Rawlins.

All the murders had been more gruesome than in any case the police had ever seen. Blade had tortured his victims before he had killed and dismembered them. He would then deposit certain body parts—a finger, a thumb, an ear—at a public place like a restaurant or mall, where it would be sure to be found.

But he had made one fatal mistake—he had killed a cop and had almost killed Symone. The media had had a field day with the case. By the time the investigation was over, the whole world had learned who Kevin Stokes alias Johnny Blade was, and they had also learned who had brought him to justice—Symone Rawlins.

That's why she wanted to be here. She wanted to look into his eyes and see fear—the same fear he had put in her.

Symone heard the sound of keys jingling outside the chamber doors. What had been whispering amongst strangers suddenly turned to dead silence.

The door to the execution chamber slowly opened. In Symone's mind, the scene resembled an old "B" movie, where the climax was happening in slow motion.

As the door opened, a huge guard escorted a shackled Johnny Blade into the room. Behind him were two more security guards. The door to the chamber closed with a hollow slam, like a door to a medieval dungeon.

There he was. Johnny Blade, murderer. Symone had never thought that she would be this close to him again. Thank God for the glass. A sudden sneer enveloped her face at the thought of crashing through the glass and ripping out Blade's heart with her bare hands. At least that way, her face would be the last thing he'd ever see.

He was directed to the chair and seated. His chest, hands and feet were strapped down tightly before his shackles were removed. Symone saw the tension finally erupting in Blade's body, as his bound hands slowly closed into tight fists. He sat immobile, trapped, about to meet his maker—whoever that was, she thought. She stared at him. She searched her mind and heart for a split second, searching for a crumb of pity. She found none.

Eye patches were applied with tape, along with a mouthpiece that was taped across his mouth. Symone's heart raced as a black hood was placed over his head. The final moment was now at hand.

After they had prepped him, the two guards stepped backed to the far wall, while the first guard took his place at the switch.

Symone stepped closer to the glass. Her chest began to heave up and down, up and down, faster than normal. Her lips parted slightly as she took in deep breaths.

Instinctively, Omar moved close to her and wrapped his arm around her shoulders. Her body trembled beneath his embrace. He glanced down at her face; a glistening tear rolled down her cheek.

The warden signaled the guard with a nod, and the switch was pulled. Above their heads, the lights flickered, affected by a brief drain of energy. Blade's body convulsed and spasmed, and then it was over—too quickly, it seemed.

Symone looked long and hard at the limp hands and drooping head of a dead man. She took a deep breath, exhaled and whispered, "It is finished."

Two

May had always been Symone's favorite month of the year. The mornings began sunny, mild, with clear blue skies. It was the perfect time in which to take a leave of absence from the department. Now that the Blade case had finally been laid to rest, Symone was enjoying some much needed R&R.

Through a screened window, a light breeze floated into Symone's two-story townhouse in downtown Baltimore. In the kitchen, she stood on a three-legged stool, reaching up to clean a white ceiling fan. She hummed and swayed to the tunes of an R. Kelly CD. Her worn-out blue jeans and tan Morgan State University sweatshirt draped her trim form comfortably. On her head, she had tied a blue and tan bandana. Symone was in her zone, as well as in her favorite pink bunny slippers.

Lately, her days had been filled with home restoration and relaxation. When she wasn't working around the house, she curled up with a good book in her best-liked antique rocker, or just lounged on her deck, enjoying the weather.

Music and house chores had been a weekend ritual for Symone ever since she could remember. Last night, she had rented old black and white videos and had sat up most of the night watching lost episodes of I Love Lucy.

Cleaning the house from top to bottom was like therapy, although her real therapy had been with a shrink downtown for the past three months.

Symone had had trouble sleeping, especially after the execution. Lately, she had had only one bad dream, as opposed to the nightly terrors she'd formerly experienced. She had dreamed that she was strapped to the electric chair and she fought to get out of it. And instead of a security guard, it was Blade who had his hand on the switch. According to Carolyn Crain, her psychotherapist, Symone still had not yet reached the core of her emotions, which might or might not be the main cause for her nightmares. But to Symone, having only one dream a week, as opposed to the normal three or four, was a blessing. She felt that the whole rest and relaxation thing was finally working.

After a long day of spring cleaning, Symone took a hot bath and settled in for the evening. She drank a cup of tea and went to bed. Dozing in and out, she awoke to her body flinching and jerking, realizing that she had been dreaming. It was the same nightmare as before.

Symone sat straight up in her bed, shaking. Sebastian, her cat, would usually make himself a comfortable spot at the foot of her bed. But this time, she awakened to find he had taken refuge in a corner chair.

As much as she wanted to think that she was getting better, Symone realized that she needed to continue her sessions with the therapist.

Sincerity in her voice, she said, "I did it again, huh, baby?" The cat cautiously jumped from the chair and pounced onto the bed. Symone cradled him and rubbed his head gently.

Sebastian purred as if to answer her question.

"I'm sorry I scared you," she said apologetically. "Mommy is starting to scare herself," Symone confessed for the first time, as she continued caressing the cat's lean body with long, slow strokes. She realized that she was far from being cured and the doctor had been right all along.

Sebastian nuzzled up against her breast and remained there the rest of the night. Symone finally drifted back to sleep.

❦

The next day, Symone found herself lying flat on her back on a leather chaise, her eyes focused on a ceiling fan hovering above.

"What's been happening since the last time we spoke, Symone?" Carolyn asked, twiddling a pen between her fingers.

Rebelliously Symone answered, "You know just as much as I do, Doctor. I suspect you kept good notes." Exposing her innermost feelings and fears still didn't sit well with Symone.

For months now, Symone had purposely avoided her lieutenant's insistence on her psychological sessions. Since Blade's execution, Symone had been relieved of her duties, and ordered to see a shrink. Naturally, she had found every excuse in the book not to go, but Symone had realized that coming a few times and talking about her emotional state did ease her mind to some degree. Last night had been an indication that she still needed Carolyn.

"Symone, there's no need to be defiant," Carolyn said, leaning back in her leather swivel chair. It had been a few months now; Carolyn was clearly used to Symone's stubbornness. "I want to get to the bottom of these bad dreams just as much as you do, but we can't make progress if you're not willing to talk to me." Her voice and demeanor were as calm and immovable as the first day Symone had set foot in the office.

As much as she respected and trusted Carolyn, Symone still had a problem discussing her personal life. She wanted everyone around her to think that she was this strong superwoman, when, in fact, she wasn't at all. She knew that under her strong, petite exterior was a woman prone to vulnerability and fragile emotions. She was no better or no stronger than the next person.

"I can tell you one thing," Carolyn said.

"What's that, Doc?"

"You have a control problem," she said, looking at Symone with piercing blue eyes. Symone felt that Carolyn could see right through her little charade. "You're so desperately trying to stay in control that you can't even see that you're driving yourself out of control."

"How do you figure that? I'm not the one out of control here. Maybe you should check out my so-called friends. They're so busy minding my business when they should be concerned about their own." Symone stuck out her chin in defiance.

Carolyn remained calm, nonchalantly jotting down notes.

"Okay, then. Why don't you tell me what you think is the matter with your friends? Why do you think they are the ones losing it?"

Closing her eyes, Symone considered her response. She took a deep breath. Putting her feelings into words seemed to be the hardest thing she found herself trying to do lately. It seemed that her entire life depended upon what she said and how she acted. She felt as if everyone had to walk lightly around her, or watch what they said to her, when all she wanted to do was work.

"How is your sex life, Symone?" Carolyn asked suddenly.

"I beg your pardon?" Symone said in surprise.

"Are you getting enough?" Carolyn persisted.

"That's none of your business. . .right?"

"In most cases, maybe. But in your case, it could help to shed some light on the dreams you've been having."

"Oh, right. Next you'll be telling me that sex alleviates headaches."

Symone's quick tongue evoked a grin from Carolyn, who rarely seemed to smile. "It has been proven, you know."

Symone shook her head. "If you must know, I don't have time for extracurricular activities. Besides, there ain't nobody in mind that I would want to do it with. Yet I still can't see what my sex life has to do with why I'm here."

"It's obvious that you're under a great deal of stress. Because stress comes in many ways, shapes, and forms, it could be a possibility that your sex life, whether active or not, can have an effect on the dreams you're having. You said it yourself. The dreams are pretty intense, frightening, and at times overpowering."

"What do my dreams have to do with sex?" Symone asked again.

"Well? Aren't all of those characteristics I just named related to sex?"

Symone sat up from the sofa and turned in Carolyn's direction. She wasn't going to say whether or not she was sexually active; she couldn't see how that could be an issue. Besides, even if she did have a man, which she didn't, she damn sure wouldn't tell it to another woman, even if she was her doctor. "Seriously, Doc. You're barking up the wrong tree. My sex life is fine."

"Okay, then. Why don't you tell me how you feel since the death of your brother and the execution of your nemesis?"

Carolyn had hit a nerve. Symone's relaxed body suddenly became tight. "What's there to talk about? They're both dead."

"What do you feel?"

Annoyed, Symone responded with clenched teeth. "One I wish I could bring back, but I can't. And the other—" she paused. "The other—I hope he's in hell. Now, is that feeling enough for you, Doctor?"

Carolyn nodded. "That's good. That's real good, Symone. Now we're starting to get somewhere."

Symone fell back onto the sofa. She sighed long and hard. She fought back the tears that had erupted in her eyes.

"What I'm trying to show you, Symone, is that it's the pain inside you that's being transformed into the nightmares. It's the pain you felt when you lost your brother. And it's the same pain you're feeling right now."

Carolyn's words cut through Symone's heart like a knife. She had thought that if she took on the blame and the guilt of Jordan's death, somehow her pretending to be "okay" would outweigh the real pain in her heart. Tears slowly rolled down the sides of her face. "That's not true. I've gotten past that."

"Then why the tears, Symone?"

Like a child, Symone tried sucking up her pain. "I don't know why I'm crying," she said, wiping away the tears. "Sometimes I do that. Is that a crime?"

"No. Let me ask you this. Have you really taken the time to release the control you forced on yourself? I want to know if you've willingly allowed yourself to mourn."

Symone frowned. "What sort of question is that? What person in their right mind is not in control of their emotions? I have to stay in control, or else—".

Calmly, Carolyn said, "Or else what? You lose it? You become human? What is it that you're afraid to surrender, Symone?"

Symone sobbed and her voice cracked. "I'm not afraid of anything. I'm a cop, for Pete's sake." Her tears again welled up in her eyes, but she fought hard to keep them from spilling down her cheeks.

"You have to stop living behind your badge, Detective. All you're doing is distancing yourself from what's really important. . .living a normal life and finally putting the past behind you."

Angrily, Symone rose from the sofa. "Do you think having the people you love struck down in the prime of their lives is normal? Do you have to watch your back to make sure someone you've put behind bars is not out to get you? Do you think having to put off a decent relationship, or avoid starting a family because you're too afraid that someday someone's going to put a bullet in you, is normal? Is that normal to you, Doctor? I don't think so. But those are the kinds of questions I find myself asking every day of my life."

Carolyn's gaze on Symone was long and empathic. "What has happened in your life is not your fault. Life didn't say it was going to be all sunshine and roses."

"That's all I hear—it's not your fault, it's not your fault. If it's not my fault that my brother was killed because of me, then tell me, Doctor, who in the hell's fault is it?" Carolyn didn't answer.

Cynically, Symone chuckled. "Like I said, it was my fault." She stood up from the sofa, reached for her belongings, and walked toward the door. "I don't care what anyone says. I was the cause of Jordan's death. I should have made him stay in the car. It should have been me, not him. He was the rookie and I should have been watching his back." Her breath seemed to get stuck in her throat. She wanted to get out of there. She needed to breathe.

"You have to train your subconscious mind to stop curs-
ing, rehearsing and nursing the pain, Symone. That's what
having a conscience is. It instructs us when we're unsure of
what to do next, but it can also enslave us if we don't know
how to let go and let God do what we can't do."

With a sarcastic grin, Symone added, "God. Where was
God when my brother was killed?"

As she opened the door, Carolyn called out to her. "Let
go of it, Symone. Please. If not for yourself, for your brother."

Turning toward Carolyn, she said, "That's a pretty tall
order for someone who has lost faith in themselves."

"Symone. If you don't remember anything else we've
discussed, remember this. Time can only move in one
direction. Your present condition will not be your destination, but I must warn you. Until you can face your demons,
you'll always be running."

Symone started to walk out, then paused for a moment.
"You said it yourself, Doc. Everything has a beginning and
an end." She defiantly threw her bag over her shoulder.
"Well, I'm about to find out what the end holds for me.
Good-bye, doctor."

Three

At the police firing range, Symone stood straddle-legged and determined; her ears were plugged and her eyes protected by glasses. She took aim at her paper target. The smoke from her 9mm Barretta filled the air as she fired rapidly, repeatedly reloading, and emptying three magazines into the paper target twenty-five yards away. After being away for two months, Symone wanted to be sure that she hadn't lost her aim. She hadn't; Symone landed every shot dead center.

She felt a sense of balance when she practiced at the firing range. She couldn't wait to get back to the daily duties of being a cop. In Symone's opinion, being a police officer kept her sharp and focused.

When she stopped to load her fourth magazine, she felt a hand tap her shoulder. Taken by surprise, she turned abruptly to see Omar, standing perfectly still behind her.

"There you are. I've been looking for you," he said.

She pushed a button and the target rapidly moved toward them. All the holes were dead center around the eight and nine rings—a perfect score.

"Damn. I think you've outscored yourself this time," Omar remarked.

"You think you can do better?" she asked, placing her gun down and removing the earplugs.

"Oh, I don't know," he said playfully. "Maybe."

"Care to put a friendly wager on it?" Symone asked with the same playful smile.

"How much you got?" he asked.

Symone looked him straight in the eye and said, "How much you willing to give up?"

Omar began to laugh. Symone knew he wasn't going to challenge her. First of all, Omar didn't gamble; secondly, she knew he didn't want it to go down in office history that a woman had outshot him.

"Maybe some other time, under different circumstances." Saving face, Omar graciously declined the challenge. "I'd rather spare you the humiliation, since it is your first week back from two months of medical leave. It would be cruel of me to have to embarrass you like that," Omar joked.

"Oh, right. Chicken," she teased.

"Sticks and stones may break my bones, but names will never hurt me."

They laughed.

Omar reached out and hugged Symone. "It's good to have you back, partner."

"It's good to be back, partner."

They exchanged smiles.

Symone placed her gun back into her holster, balled up the paper target and tossed it toward the trash can. She missed. "Dammit," she cursed.

"Let me show you how it's done." Omar walked over, picked up the crumpled paper, came back, stood beside her and tossed the paper. It went directly in the trash can. "See? It's all in the wrist," he said, turning his hand.

Smiling, she rolled her eyes at him and said, "Oh, give me a break."

"You still seeing that shrink?"

"Nope." She saw the surprised look on his face.

"Why not?"

Charlene A. Berry

"Because there's nothing wrong with me that a little hard work can't cure. Besides, I want to be here. I need to be here. Aren't you glad I'm back?"

"Yeah. You're my partner."

"Then that's all that matters." Symone walked away, heading back to the station.

Omar glanced at her from the corner of his eye. "Hey," he called out to her.

Symone turned to him.

"I'm proud of you, kid," he said with a smile.

❈ ☻ ❈

By the crack of dawn, Symone had already worked up a vigorous sweat. Before 9 a.m., she had kicked and punched her way through an early-morning workout.

Turning one of her three bedrooms into a personal gym had been Jordan's idea. But now it belonged to Symone.

Behind the swaying leather body-bag stood Toni Campbell, Symone's workout partner and good friend. She held the bag as Symone forcefully attacked it. Symone's sweaty palms, feet and knuckles made a permanent imprint in the bag.

"Hold still!" Symone yelled.

"You stop kicking it so damned hard, then!" Toni yelled back.

Hitting the bag with her knee, Symone stepped back and kicked it, knocking Toni into a wall.

"Arrr! That's it, I quit!" Toni screamed, hugging her body. "What are you trying to do? Kill me?"

Symone huffed and puffed exhaustedly. She stared at her friend. "Okay, I'll give you a five-minute break."

"Five minutes, hell. I said I quit. Q-U-I-T. Quit."

Symone nodded her head and chuckled at Toni's bitching.

"You need to work out less," Toni complained, staggering to the windowsill to rest. "All this sweating and kicking you be doing...I can think of a whole lot of other ways to expend the kind of energy you're putting out. And it doesn't require all this jungle gym stuff, either."

Symone, still breathing hard, picked up a liter of water. Looking at Toni, she gulped it down. "Ahhh. Good," she said, wiping water from the corners of her mouth. "I can't imagine what it could be."

"Honey, all you need is a man and a soft place to lay." Toni devilishly raised an eyebrow. "You'd be amazed how good you'll feel after you both work out together."

"Oh! I suppose you want me to believe that that's how you keep your weight under control?"

Toni held her arms outstretched and turned full circle. "Do you see any flab?"

Symone tapped her pointer finger on the side of Toni's head. "Yeah. Right here," she said with a giggle.

Toni brushed away Symone's hand. "I'm serious, Symone. You haven't had a date in God knows how long. What are you trying to do, become a member of the 'Lonely Hearts Club' or something?"

"Or something." Symone picked up a towel. "Look, would you like some iced tea?" She turned and walked out of the room.

Toni slowly followed Symone downstairs to the kitchen. "C'mon, Symone. When was the last time you went out with a guy? And I don't mean with your cop friends, either. I'm talking about a real man."

Symone poured the tea into glasses without uttering a word. Her eyes were on the brown liquid flowing into the glass.

Charlene A. Berry

"You have no idea, do you?" Toni asked, looking directly at Symone's face.

"What difference does it make? I don't measure who I am on the basis of having a man in my life. Or in my bed, for that matter. I mean, what's the big deal, anyway?"

Toni placed her hand on top of Symone's before she could sit down. "Oh my God. Has it been that long?"

Symone snatched her hand from under Toni's and sat down at the table. They both sat silently for a moment.

"Last week, my therapist asked me that same question," Symone said at last. "Well, not exactly the way you said it, but close enough. She said that my dreams could possibly be linked to me not getting any. Can you believe that?" Symone tried to make light of Carolyn's words.

"And she's right," Toni added.

"Oh, what do you know?" Symone felt just as defiant toward Toni as she had with Carolyn.

"So you're still having the dreams, and you're not cured?"

"It's gonna take a little more time, I guess."

"You guess? You guess? Symone, the dreams are all in your head, Baby. You can stop them if you want to."

Symone's voice escalated. "Don't you think if I could do that I would have done it a long time ago? You think I enjoy going to bed scared out of my mind? Is that what you think?" She abruptly pushed herself away from the table, walked to the sink and sobbed.

Toni got up. She moved toward her friend and wrapped her arms around Symone from behind. "I'm sorry. I didn't mean to upset you."

"It's not you. It's me. It's always been me. Ever since Jordan died, it's been real hard to let go."

"But you can." Toni turned Symone's face toward her. "You're not alone. There's nothing you should be going through by yourself. That's what friends are for. The ones who love you the most are still here. I'm here—all the time. You can't get rid of me."

Symone laughed. "You're crazy, you know that? But you're right and Carolyn is right. The one thing that scares me the most is having to spend the rest of my life alone. It's funny. I never realized, until Jordan died, how risky a relationship is for me. What if I do get involved with a man and something happens to me? You can't possibly imagine the pain I'd put the guy through. But I can't just quit my job. Being a cop is who I am. And what about children? Do you know how hard it is to grow up without a mother?" Symone slammed her hand down on the countertop. "That's what I'm afraid of. Leaving people that I love behind to suffer the same way I've suffered this past year. That's not love...that's cruelty."

Toni pulled Symone into her arms. "The only cruel thing I see is you not giving yourself a chance to love and be loved. Symone, you got so much love to give that it scares you. But that's what love is. It's about taking chances. And believe me, when you do meet the right guy, you'll have everything you need."

Four

It had been five days since her return to the job, and Symone had worked harder these last couple of days than she had worked her whole eight years on the force.

"Well, well, well. Look who's working through her lunch hour," Cortez, the station's self-proclaimed Casanova, said as he stood in front of Symone's desk. "What's the matter, Rawlins, you couldn't find a date for lunch?" His Spanish accent was heavy.

She halted her paperwork and gave him a cool grin. "No. But I guess you would know all about missed dates. From what I heard, your last one couldn't make it because you didn't have an air pump to blow her up."

Even with Symone's show of cockiness, Cortez continued to tread upon dangerous ground. Glancing back at his fellow colleagues, he grinned. "Okay. I'll give you that one, Rawlins. But tell me. When was the last time you had a real man?" he asked, grabbing his crotch.

Symone frowned at his idiotic male-chauvinist behavior. She wanted to teach him a lesson and deflate his ego at the same time. She gave Omar a warning glance not to interfere, then stood up, walked around the desk, and put her face directly in Cortez'. Suddenly, she grabbed his balls and squeezed. He screeched like a girl. "Oh! And here I thought you were a man," Symone said, releasing her grip on him. She chuckled and whispered into Cortez' ear. "Don't ever try to embarrass me like that again."

Snickers fell from the lips of her fellow officers as they listened in amusement. In seconds, laughter filled the station.

Symone knew that of all the men who might cruelly tease her, Cortez would be the most likely one. He had been trying to sleep with her since his transfer to the district.

As loudly as the laughter escalated, the volume of sound was topped by the slam of Lieutenant Spaulding's office door.

"I hope I'm paying you all to work, and not for leisurely standing around." Lieutenant Spaulding's hard gaze ignited a fire beneath his unit; they all rushed back to their duties. "Rawlins and Harris." His voice thundered with authority. "Into my office, now."

The other officers abruptly stopped their work and stared, while Symone and Omar hurried through the lieutenant's door. They weren't in their chairs before Spaulding began to speak. "I just got off the phone with Commissioner Wells. He just got off the phone with the commissioner of New Orleans," he said, sitting behind a large wooden desk. "There's big trouble brewing down in the bayous."

Symone and Omar looked at each other questioningly.

"I was asked—no, let me rephrase that," Spaulding said. "I was ordered to send two of my best men to New Orleans to help with the investigation. It seems that New Orleans got themselves a killer whose MO is exactly like the Blade case."

"With no disrespect, sir," Omar said as he leaned toward the desk. "What does this have to do with us? We got no jurisdiction down South."

Spaulding reached under a pile of reports and slid a folder across his desk to Omar. "We do now."

Omar opened the folder; Symone leaned over to take a glance. The pictures were of slaughtered victims, and they blew her away. She had thought that she would never again have to see bodies this mutilated. Fear gripped her gut as her mind went back to Blade. She suddenly felt light-headed. A chill ran down her spine.

"The suspect's MO is the same as our own Johnny Blade. The only twist is the killer carves some sort of symbol into the victims' skin," Spaulding said. He reached out and snatched an incoming fax from the fax machine beside his desk.

Symone clutched the pictures in her hand. Her nails almost pierced the paper. The blood, the carvings, the bits of flesh scattered throughout the photos caused her blood to run cold through her veins. Her heart began to palpitate.

Reluctantly, she peered more closely at the photos, studying the odd carving that appeared on every corpse. Two identical markings side by side—II. "Do they know what these symbols mean?" she asked.

Spaulding shrugged. "They've guessed they're the killer's initials. Or Roman numerals. But they're pretty much in the dark."

Omar looked up suspiciously from the pictures. "But, again, Lieutenant: What does this have to do with us? If they need help, why don't they call the feds?"

"The FBI is involved. As a matter of fact, they've sent one of their best forensic psychologists down there. Agent La'Mon. Josiah La'Mon." He handed Symone a photo of Agent La'Mon and his bio, which had just come over the fax. "He will be your contact person in New Orleans."

The black and white photo captured Symone's attention immediately. Her eyes widened as she scanned the photo intently. La'Mon's strong facial structure—the broad nose, the high cheekbones, and the mysteriousness of his oddly shaped, slanted eyes—momentarily held Symone captive. Obviously there were Asian ancestors mixed with his African lineage.

"A Profiler?" she said, handing the picture over to Omar.

"From what I've heard, he's the best. Commissioner Wells seems to think so," Spaulding said.

"I think I heard of this guy, or at least read about him somewhere. I don't remember where," Symone said.

"So, to reiterate the question," Omar said, "what does this case have to do with us?"

"Because you have experience with serial killers, particularly ones who do that to their victims." Spaulding pointed to the photos and then fumbled through some files on his desk. "From what I hear, La'Mon has already painted a picture of who the killer might be."

Symone licked her lips and compressed them together in a rigid line. "I know what a profiler is and I also know what they do, Lieutenant. But the question still remains: What makes us prime candidates for this case?"

"From what the commissioner has told me, La'Mon read about the Blade case and was impressed with how well it was handled," he said, opening a drawer to his desk. "In fact, he was so impressed that he hand-picked both of you personally." Spaulding handed Symone and Omar two plane tickets. "Your plane leaves tomorrow. Need I say more?"

☾ ☻ ☽

The evening skies darkened with a purplish hue, and a cool breeze floated through the tops of the trees. Symone stood shivering in the doorway of her balcony wearing a silk lace robe. The evening air grazed her body as she walked out onto the balcony, her arms folded across her chest. She gazed at the hazy, iridescent blue light surrounding the twenty-story Braum Seltzer clock, which seemed to be standing in the middle of Harbor Place. It showed eleven o'clock.

Her thoughts floated along with the breeze. She attempted not to think about New Orleans, or the trouble they were having. The last thing she needed was another homicide, especially a multiple one. But this time it was different. At least she had a chance to get out of town. Although New Orleans was not her favorite vacation spot, she looked forward to enjoying some warmer weather. She doubted that she'd find the time to take in the sights, but anything was better than the chill that had blanketed Baltimore city for the third week in a row.

She thought of encountering new places and faces, especially one face in particular—Agent La'Mon's. Suddenly, her thoughts were interrupted by the phone.

Walking bare-footed across the thick carpet, she picked up the receiver on the third ring. "Hello."

High-pitched bells and sirens in the background drowned out the voice on the other end of the phone.

Raising her voice, Symone said again, "Hello!"

"Symone. It's Omar. Can you hear me?"

"Barely. Where are you?"

In a loud voice, Omar said, "I'm at the emergency room. An ambulance just arrived with a car accident victim."

The sirens in the background faded away. "What are you doing at a hospital this time of night, Omar?"

Voice shaking, Omar said, "It's Monica. She started spotting late this evening." Symone could hear him more clearly now.

She gasped. "Omar. Oh, no. I'm sorry to hear that." She knew how much this pregnancy meant to Omar. Monica was four months pregnant. "Is she okay? She didn't lose the baby, did she?"

"No. Thank God. As far as we know, the baby's fine."

"Thank goodness. Is the doctor going to keep her overnight?"

"They're contemplating it, since this is our first baby. I just don't want to leave her alone."

"Omar. That shouldn't even be an option. Your place is beside your wife and child."

"But, Symone..."

"No buts! Your only concern is being there with Monica. There is nothing outside of birthing and raising a healthy baby, man."

"But, Symone, the lieutenant is expecting both of us on that plane tomorrow morning."

With a firm voice, Symone said, "I'll be on that plane tomorrow. You, on the other hand, have a wife and a little baby to worry about."

"But this case needs the both of us. You can't expect me to let you go to New Orleans alone, can you?"

Symone was determined not to let Omar talk her out of making the trip without him. "Yes," she insisted. "And not another word. Once your wife is stronger, you can catch up with me in New Orleans."

Symone could hear the calmness return to Omar's voice. "You're something else. You know that?"

Smiling at his remark, Symone said, "I'll try to remember that when I'm face to face with the psychopath."

Five

When the plane landed at New Orleans International Airport at 12:45 p.m., Symone stepped out of the comfort of an air-conditioned Boeing 767 into lovely 85 degree weather—at least that's what the TelePrompTer displayed as she walked through the terminal.

Symone knew she looked pretty snazzy in a taupe skirt with a white silk blouse, tan heels and shoulder bag. She wanted to make her first impression a lasting one.

As the conveyer belt at the luggage claim area spun around, Symone reached down and picked up her small suitcase. She had thought of packing more, but she was hoping that her stay in New Orleans would be brief.

The rays from the sun outside the terminal seemed brighter and hotter than on any day she had experienced lately in Baltimore. Squinting, she approached the glare coming from beyond the revolving glass doors. Slipping a pair of dark Prada shades on her face, she stepped out into the Cajun heat.

A wide smile enveloped her face as she tilted her head toward the sun. "Mmm. This is more like it. Plenty of sunshine and fresh air, all that a girl needs."

She looked to her left and then to her right; she saw no sign of her contact person. She gripped the handle on her suitcase more tightly; the thought of being forgotten did enter her head. With more than a thousand people floating around the airport, she knew no one and, what was worse, no one knew her.

"Okay," she mumbled under her breath. "Where the hell are you, La'Mon?" She glanced down at her watch, then abruptly looked up, scanning the view in every direction.

She thought she heard someone calling her name. But in the commotion and the noise outside the airport—the blaring taxi horns, the constant chatter of travelers moving to and fro—she might have been mistaken.

Pacing along the sidewalk, she kept her eyes and ears open nonetheless. It was not easy for her to stay calm; her stomach had butterflies in it. Maybe it was just her nerves, she thought. The thought of being left behind could shake anybody up. Smiling, she thought about her and Omar's last conversation, how overprotective he had been. He acted more like an older brother than a partner. If only she did have a man like that in her life, who didn't act like a brother or a partner, but like a lover. Symone could count with one finger how many relationships she had had. She prayed that one day those odds would change drastically.

Symone sighed, becoming more and more nervous. There was a slim possibility that Agent La'Mon had forgotten to pick her up.

She pulled a tissue from her purse and blotted the perspiration off her brow. The heat was more intense than she had at first realized, and the Deep South humidity was oppressive.

Suddenly, out of nowhere, a voice began bellowing her name. "Symone! Symone, darling. There you are."

The voice was unfamiliar to her. She stood peering through the crowd of pedestrians. She couldn't see who was calling out to her. Could it be Agent La'Mon? If so, why in the world would he be calling her darling?

As the crowd around her thinned, Symone caught a glimpse of what looked like La'Mon but, with the distance

Charlene A. Berry

between them, she still wasn't sure. She was hoping it was Agent La'Mon for two reasons: one, she wanted to get out of the heat that was wreaking havoc on her skin, and two, she wanted to relieve her aching feet.

As the stranger grew closer, Symone saw that he was not her contact man. Agent La'Mon had been clean-shaven in his photograph. The man coming in her direction had a mustache and goatee. He wore a large hat, which barely covered his dreadlocks.

The stranger's build seemed thicker than La'Mon's. He had broad shoulders. His face was hidden behind a pair of dark sunglasses. He walked as if he were in a hurry. Symone wasn't sure who he was, but one thing she was sure of—it wasn't Agent La'Mon.

Carefully reaching her hand into her purse, she gripped the snub-nose .38 revolver she carried for backup. She had to be ready for anything.

When the stranger was within arm's reach, he stretched out his arms and embraced Symone tightly. The strength of his hug was sudden but somehow genuine. "Do not be alarmed, Detective," he whispered in her ear. "I'm Agent La'Mon, your contact."

Symone widened her eyes in silent concern, but she did not relinquish her grip on her gun.

Agent La'Mon said, "Just play along. Act as if we know each other." Then he kissed her passionately on the lips.

Overwhelmed with surprise again, Symone was unable to speak as his tongue abruptly parted her tight lips. She was thrown for a loop by Agent La'Mon's actions and caught off guard by his kiss. The lip-locking event seemed to last forever, though it lasted only seconds. The kiss was good, she thought, as her nipples hardened and her knees weakened. She could taste the sweetness of cinnamon on his lips.

Symone was still in a daze as Agent La'Mon released his hold on her and quickly ushered her to his waiting silver Mustang GT convertible.

Symone tried to push him away, but Josiah La'Mon held her close. He had rendered her speechless for the moment. Now the butterflies in her stomach felt more like crazed rabbits jumping around. She didn't know whether to slap him, or just stand there awestruck. Her heart pounded rapidly in her chest and she broke out in a sweat.

With a scowl, she demanded through clenched teeth, "What in the hell do you think you're doing?" Josiah had done something no man had ever done to Symone before, unravel her senses. Never had any of her cases started out this way, and she doubted very seriously that they would ever end the same way. "I demand to see some I.D."

"I'd rather wait until we get into the car, sweetheart." Symone could tell that he wasn't going to do anything until they both were safely in the car.

He gently pulled her by the arm. Symone didn't want to cause a scene so she gave in to his haste.

Josiah popped the trunk and tossed her suitcase into it. He walked around, opened the car door and helped her in. Once behind the wheel, he peeled rubber and they left the airport.

Symone scowled at the dark, tinted windows, then turned her fury on Josiah. She pulled out her gun and aimed it at him. "Goddammit, if you don't produce some ID right now, I'm gonna put a bullet in your knee."

Instantly, Josiah swerved to the side of the road, jammed the car into park and aggressively turned to Symone. He started to reach into his pocket.

"Nice and easy," she said.

Josiah reached his hand into his back pocket. "You can put the gun away. That won't be necessary."

Charlene A. Berry

"I'll be the judge of that, thank you." Symone sat with her back against the car door as he handed her his wallet. She barely took her eyes off him. She flipped the wallet open with one hand, holding her gun in the other. "You look nothing like your picture."

"If you'll just give me a minute to explain."

She gritted her teeth. "You have two seconds,"

Josiah began to pull off his mustache and the goatee. They were fake, but good. He then took off the sunglasses and the hat. The dreadlocks wig was attached to the hat. "Now, take another look. Do you recognize me now, Detective? Is this better?"

Symone gasped with surprise. His face was beautiful. His disguise had been very good...so good that he had had Symone fooled.

"I wouldn't say better." Symone shyly turned her head to keep from smiling. He had gotten one over on her, and nobody had ever done that.

Josiah grinned as he drove the car back onto the road. Even his eyes were brighter than they had seemed in his photo. She thought that his photograph didn't do him justice. Her contact man was indeed handsome, not to mention full of surprises.

"So why the disguise and that kiss?"

"The disguise is for protection," Josiah said.

Symone shook her head in bewilderment. "Protection? From whom?"

"We don't know yet. As you may have been briefed, we have a killer on the loose who has, so far, been two steps ahead of us. Several of our officers have already been the targets of attack."

"No one said anything about the police being targeted."

"That's not quite the case, Detective. But there have been some close calls. Don't ask me how, but from the various descriptions we received from countless eyewitnesses, our suspect is a master of disguises."

"You think there's a leak within the department?"

"It's hard to say. But I'm not ready to accuse anyone until I can get some conclusive evidence," Josiah said, glancing at her.

"You referred to the suspect as 'he'. We're looking for a man?"

"Well, I'll use that term loosely. The descriptions we've gotten so far have been of a white male, in his late twenties, early thirties. Now, there have been other reports of a woman fitting the same description."

"Are you telling me that there are two killers on the loose?"

"I hope not," he said, with a raised brow. "I believe it's one person with many disguises. Nevertheless, we've put out an all points bulletin on the two."

"Hmm," Symone said, turning her attention to the vast farmland outside the car window. "What about the kiss?" she said, turning again in his direction.

A wicked smile spread across his face. "That was merely part of the act. I had to make sure our encounter looked believable."

Symone saw a strange twinkle in his eye. She gathered the kiss had been for his benefit only, not for whoever might be watching. Secretly, she was pleased that he had found her attractive enough to do what he had done.

Josiah glanced at her. "Don't take it personally."

"Oh, I didn't," she said, with a sly grin. Briefly, they drove in silence. Then she asked: "Now that we got the formalities out of the way, you care to tell me why you requested me for this case?"

"I like your style, Detective."

"My style?"

"Yeah. I read up on the Blade case. You're quite the hero in Maryland."

Symone chuckled. "I'm no hero."

"Your bio sure makes you look like one."

"The city is relieved that the nightmare is finally over," she said, the sound of finality in her voice.

"After I read the details of the case on the Internet, I knew you were the one for this investigation. I still don't know all the details of how you caught your man, but I'm sure it wasn't easy."

"No, it wasn't. A lot of people suffered because of it," she said solemnly.

"How did you catch him, again?"

Symone didn't answer him right away. She stared out the car window. The last thing she wanted to do was bring up painful memories. From out of the corner of her eye, she noticed he was looking at her.

"You don't have to answer, you know." he said.

Glancing at him soberly, she said, "I know. But I'll tell you anyway. One day, I got a call at the station. When I answered the phone, all I heard was laughing on the other end. When the laughing stopped, he told me how thrilled he was that he had killed the cop who was my brother, you know. He then went on to say how unfortunate it was that he didn't get me." Symone felt the rage pulsating inside her chest. "I knew it was Blade."

"Why didn't you alert someone?"

"Because he made it personal. I couldn't tell anyone, not even my partner. The thought of Blade getting satisfaction from my pain, was too much. He had to be stopped."

"So, what did you do?"

"The only thing I could do: Give him another crack at me. He wanted me and I damn sure wanted him. I couldn't bear to see him living out one more day."

"You took a great risk, you know that, right?"

"I know that, now."

"Then what did you do?" he said.

"I met him on his turf. I didn't call for backup. We met at an old empty warehouse on the other side of town. I proved to him that I was unarmed and he led me inside the building at gun point." Symone saw the disbelief in Agent La'Mon's face as she told the story.

"And then what happened?"

"He told me to strip down to my underwear and get on my knees." Symone assumed, by the sudden twitch of La'Mon's eyebrow, that he was attempting to picture her in her underwear. "He told me to beg for mercy. When I was down on my knees, I tried to remember all the things I wouldn't get to do, and the people I wouldn't get to save from this monster. But most of all—" She chuckled. "This might sound crazy. I thought about the ocean. I thought that I would never get the chance to see just how blue the water really is." Symone felt the tears well up behind her eyes. She quickly blinked them away. "Anyway, he slowly began walking toward me. I could smell the stench of death on him. I saw how his eyes crept across my body. That's when I knew I had only one chance to stop him. I slowly reached up and unsnapped my bra. I knew if I could hold his attention for a few more minutes, I'd have him right where I wanted. It was working. His eyes were locked on my breasts. I smiled at him and gave him a sexy stare. I could see he was wavering in his thoughts. He didn't know whether to shoot me or screw me. I knelt there hoping for a brief window of opportunity."

La'Mon licked his lips. "And did you get it? That window of opportunity, I mean?"

"Yep. As he slowly stepped toward me, he didn't realize that he had lowered his weapon. I made sure his eyes never left me. And when I got the chance, I reached behind my back and snatched my backup revolver from my underpants, and I shot him. Twice. Once in the shoulder and once in the knee."

"Then what did you do?"

"First of all, I made sure he wasn't going anywhere. Second, I put my clothes back on, and third, I went back to my car and called for backup. And well, you know the rest."

"I sure do. In the end, justice prevailed," he said, taking a deep breath.

Symone sighed. "I doubt the families of the victims think so. No one can bring back their loved ones."

"Well, in case you're wondering," he said in a lighter tone, "you don't have to worry about stripping down for anyone here. Here, we do things together."

She realized he was trying to lighten the mood. "I'll keep that in mind, Agent La'Mon," she said, with a friendly smile.

Six

The French Quarter Hotel on Bourbon Street was one of the finest hotels on the block. With its colonial-style and pastel pink exterior, the hotel glowed with an old-fashioned charm.

New Orleans was exactly how Symone had imagined it would be. The sights and sounds, the unmistakable scent of seafood, and the smell of the Mississippi River, all danced around her senses. The only thing missing was Omar. She thought about giving him a call once she got to her room.

After she checked in, Symone asked if she had received any messages. She was a bit disappointed to find that not even Omar or her lieutenant had called to see if she had even made it there safely. No matter. She knew she would hear from them sooner or later.

Receiving her door key, Symone walked to the elevator and got on. She took the elevator up to the sixth floor and got off on a brightly lit hallway. Inserting the key card, Symone opened the door and was startled by someone inside the room. "I didn't realize that this room was taken," she gasped.

An equally startled young white woman came from within the walk-in coat closet. Her bright red hair was piled on top of her head, and she peered at Symone through thick tortoise-shell glasses. "I'm sorry. I wasn't aware that this room was booked so soon. I was instructed to clean the room."

Symone gave her a friendly grin. "Don't rush on my account. I'm just getting here myself. Take your time."

The housekeeper hurried to complete her work, while Symone busied herself by checking out the room. She was more than pleased with her accommodations. The NOPD had spared no expense in showing their hospitality. Symone's room was actually a suite.

Unlocking the glass sliding door to the balcony, Symone opened it and walked out. She took a deep breath and exhaled slowly. Strangely enough, she felt welcome here.

"If you don't mind me asking, ma'am," the housekeeper said, standing at the threshold of the balcony. "Are you visiting N'awlins for pleasure or business?"

Symone turned. "Business. Hopefully I'll be able sneak in a little bit of pleasure, if I can."

"If you need a guide, ma'am, I'll be happy to show you around."

"That's really nice of you...uh..." Symone was trying to read the name badge on the woman's white uniform.

Wiping her hand on her dress, she extended it to Symone. "Tina, ma'am. Tina Fisk."

Symone shook the young woman's hand firmly and felt an answering strong pressure from Tina. "I'm Symone Rawlins. Glad to meet you."

With a gasp, Tina suddenly jerked as if the handshake had shocked her. Her legs buckled beneath her.

With quick reflexes, Symone reached out, grabbed Tina by the hand and assisted her to a nearby chair. She saw that Tina was disoriented.

"Let me get you some water." Symone rushed into the kitchen and hurried back with a glass of water. She handed it to Tina, who drank it down slowly.

Symone knelt in front of her. "Would you like me to call down to the front desk?"

With a strain in her voice, Tina said, "No. I'm fine, ma'am. This happens all the time, but never this intense."

Symone was bewildered by the young woman's response. "I don't understand. Are you ill?"

Tina gave a one-sided smile and tucked a stray red curl into her top knot. "No. I'm not ill. At times, some people would like to think so. They're afraid of what they do not understand."

"You've lost me. They're afraid of what?"

"My curse. Or my blessing, as my grandma used to put it."

Symone gave Tina a questioning look. She thought the young woman was very strange.

"I'm psychic. At least, that's the fancy term for it. The old ones call it soothsaying."

Symone looked at Tina skeptically. She didn't believe in black magic or people with so-called psychic powers, but was willing hear the woman out. "How did you become...?"

"Psychic? As far as I can remember, I've been like this since I was a little girl. You'd think people would understand, at least accept it openly."

Symone had always considered herself to be open-minded, but this hocus-pocus stuff was far beyond normal.

"When I touched your hand," Tina continued, "I saw strange images in my head. They were all jumbled-like."

"Forgive me if I seem skeptical, but I don't believe in that sort of stuff."

"I didn't, either. But the more it kept happening to me, the more I had to understand why. So, whenever it did, I tried to harness it, control it."

Symone stood up and walked to her suitcase. She couldn't believe she was standing here listening to such foolishness.

Tina stood up slowly. "I could read your cards for you, if you like." She reached into her uniform pocket and pulled' out a deck of cards with a rubber band around it. She walked to the table and sat down.

Symone stood waiting for a moment, wanting the young woman to leave, but she finally sat down at the table to humor Tina.

Tina spread the cards face down on the table in a fan formation. "Pick out seven cards and give them to me."

Symone hesitated. She chuckled at the thought of going this far with what she considered a foolish game. She picked out one card, then two more, then four more.

Tina slid the remainder of the cards to the side, took the seven cards Symone had picked out and began to turn them over, one by one. The first card revealed a woman sitting on a throne. "This card represents justice. You respect and uphold the law to the very letter," Tina said. Her gaze met Symone's, who was shocked to hear Tina say what she already knew.

Tina continued with the next card. It was the Hanged Man. "This represents letting go, suspension and sacrifice," she said, glancing at Symone. "Why are you fighting with yourself, ma'am?"

Symone's eyes widened at the question. With a blank stare, she said, "I don't know what you mean, Tina."

Tina placed the card directly beside the first drawn card.

"Let me put it another way. Why are you still blaming yourself for the past? It's time you let go of the pain, the bitterness, the anger."

Symone gasped. She knew exactly what Tina meant now. Yes, she had tried to deny what she felt. She had found a clever way of covering up that which refused to stay buried. Tears began to form in her eyes.

Pulling out a piece of tissue from her pocket, Tina handed it to Symone, who took it and dabbed her eyes.

Turning over the next card, Tina said, "The Hermit." She slid the card next to the previous one. "You are on a dangerous quest," she said.

Symone didn't flinch. She didn't want to let the woman know she was right.

"You're in search of something or someone." Again, all Symone could do was look and listen with amazement. "Be very careful," Tina warned. "What you seek is seeking you."

Symone felt her body tighten as the truth was laid out on the table. Well, what Tina proclaimed to be the truth anyway, Symone thought, forcing herself to look at the situation rationally.

Then Tina turned up the dreaded card of death. Symone didn't need an interpretation. She knew evil when she saw it.

"Okay. I think I heard enough." Symone pushed away from the table and stood up. "I don't mean to be rude, but all this stuff..." She waved her hands in air. "I don't believe in it, and neither should you."

Tina frowned, her eyes troubled behind her glasses. "This is not a game. What I told you is true, and you know it."

Symone tried to deflect the woman's perceptive remark. "Yeah, the Easter bunny and the bogeyman, they're 'true' too," she said with a sarcastic chuckle. "Look. You seem like a sweet girl. If you're doing this for money, here..." Symone reached into her pocket and pulled out some bills.

"I don't want your money, ma'am," Tina said, pushing Symone's hand back.

Symone saw the hurt in the young woman's eyes. "Look, don't take this personally, Tina. I don't believe in illusions and trickery. The only thing I believe in is me and my ability to do what is right."

"If that's how you feel, I understand. But at least let's finish what we started." Tina turned over the remaining cards, calling out the name of each: "Strength, The Tower, The Chariot and the last one, Love."

"At last!" Symone exclaimed with a grin. "There's something I haven't seen in a while. Love."

Tina picked up the cards. "True love will find you. But it will not come easy."

Laughing, Symone said, "Love! After what you've just revealed to me? Do you think I will have time to find love? Yeah, right."

"I didn't say you will find love. I said love will find you."

Symone's mood was one of skepticism. She had more important things to think about...like catching a killer.

Tina got up from the table, gathered her cards and put them back into her uniform pocket.

Symone hunched her shoulders casually. "Thanks for...the reading. It was a very interesting meeting, and entertaining." She kept the conversation light. She didn't want Tina to pull out a Ouija board next.

Symone escorted her to the door. "This was very interesting, to say the least."

Tina crossed the threshold of the door, and turned to Symone. "I hope you enjoy your stay here. Remember, don't always believe what you see. What you think you see will be but a poor reflection of what is not seen."

Symone let Tina's heartfelt words go in one ear and out the other. "Thanks. I'll try to remember that." Extending her hand, Symone suddenly remembered the last time Tina had shaken her hand. Instead, they both opted for a wave good-bye.

Tina pulled from her pocket the card of Love and gave it to Symone. "Remember, love conquers all."

⟨ ◉ ⟩

At NOPD, it seemed to be business as usual. The blaring sirens, the criminals coming and going, made Symone feel right at home.

Josiah La'Mon took her inside the office of Lieutenant Francis DeClaud.

When they walked through the door of the lieutenant's office, the pungent smell of cigar smoke hit Symone in the face. DeClaud was puffing away, standing behind his desk and talking on the telephone.

A man of average height and build, with pale, pinkish skin, DeClaud looked to be in his late fifties. He had mixed gray hair at his temples, heavy bags beneath his eyes, and a pudgy nose. He looked a bit like an aging J.R. Ewing minus the Ewing money. Instead of fat pockets of money, DeClaud had a fat belly and a bad tailor.

Closing the door behind them, Josiah and Symone each took a seat on the opposite side of DeClaud's gray metal desk.

Continuing with his conversation on the phone, the lieutenant sat down and began pecking at his computer keyboard on the corner of his desk, his cigar loosely hanging from his mouth. He seemed to be sending and receiving criminal profiles over the Net.

Symone watched silently as he conducted his business, not once looking in their direction. She already considered him rude for not acknowledging either of them.

When DeClaud ended his telephone conversation, he didn't turn in their direction right away, but completed what he was doing on the computer. At last he said, "Detective Roche'tte, I presume?" His attention was still on the information being e-mailed to him. He finally turned in his chair and sat back, as if he were waiting for Symone to take the floor.

"No, sir. It's Rawlins. But nice to meet you, anyway." Symone stood up and extended her hand to him.

Again, DeClaud took his time in accepting it. "I hope your flight was satisfactory?" His southern drawl was evident, but his hospitality needed some work. "You got quite a grip there, little lady," he remarked.

"Thank you, sir." Symone kept repeating in her head what Tina had said earlier: 'Don't believe everything you see.' She was hoping that there was more to this rude man than met the eye.

"I take it you've met Detective La' Mon already?"

She glanced at Josiah. "Yes, sir. I have."

"Good. I like to get all the formalities out of the way first before we proceed."

Throughout the briefing, Symone tried to appear comfortable in her new surroundings, but she realized her new superior wasn't going to make this transition easy on her. She thought how good it would be to see a friendly face...a face like Omar's. Just then, Lieutenant DeClaud asked about the very thing she had been thinking.

"I thought it was two of you who would be included in this investigation."

"It was, originally. But Detective Harris was called away on an emergency."

DeClaud smirked. "Maybe it's for the best. Like we say in N'awlins, 'too many hands can tip the pot,'" he said, attempting to be funny. "As pretty as you are, what do you know about catching bad guys, little lady? You should be somewhere getting your nails and hair done, not running around trying to do a man's job."

Symone frowned. She took DeClaud's pompous attitude personally. Not only did he imply that she couldn't do her job, but he had the nerve to suggest that she was better off somewhere pampering herself. The nerve of him! Symone immediately responded to his remark with a sharp retort: "You must have me confused with someone else. Perhaps a lady in your life." She saw how his facial expression change from smugness to irritation. "But you're right, I am a lady. But more importantly, I'm a cop and a damn good one. And, as far as my abilities go, anything you can do, I can do—better." Symone really wanted to give him a piece of her mind, but because she was the new kid on the block, she thought she'd wait—at least for a few more days.

"Little lady, you have a lot to learn about the South, now." His Louisiana drawl was taking its painful toll on her ears.

"For the record, Lieutenant. I've never lost a case, and I damn sure didn't come all the way down here to start now." The determination in her voice caused DeClaud to sit up and take notice; from the corner of her eye, Symone saw a slight jump from Josiah as well. "And also, don't call me little lady. Don't let my size fool you."

DeClaud wilted in his chair. Symone's abrupt reply had zapped some of the bite out of his obnoxious demeanor.

Clearing his throat, DeClaud seemed to choose his words more carefully. "Well, all I have to say is we're not

paying you to sit around and watch. This case is the worst
this state has ever seen. Now, if you can't handle it—"

"Please," she said, condescendingly. "Like I told Agent
La'Mon earlier. I'm here to do a job and do it well. I would-
n't be here if I didn't think we couldn't catch the killer. I've
been in worse scenarios and this one is no problem."

DeClaud attempted to swallow his arrogance.
"Uh...well, Agent La'Mon, you can fill her in on the rest.
So, if you'll excuse me," he said, brushing them both off, "I
have some phone calls to make."

Annoyed with DeClaud's cavalier approach, Symone
rolled her eyes, sprung from her seat and stormed out of
the office. She decided to wait for Josiah just outside the
door.

"Agent La'Mon," DeClaud said to Josiah.

"Yes, sir?"

DeClaud handed Josiah a file. "Make sure she knows
her place, and she does not get in my way."

From where she stood, Symone saw and heard everything.

Josiah snatched the folder from DeClaud, glaring at the
fat, sloppy man. "And don't you get in mine, Lieutenant."

Once outside the building, Symone marched angrily to
the car, ignoring Josiah.

"Hey, wait up!" Josiah called out.

Furiously, she paced back and forth in front of the car.
"Is he always that friendly, or was he trying to get on my
good side?" Her nostrils flared and her body temperature
seemed to outmatch the temperature outside.

Josiah walked to Symone. He put his hands on her
shoulders and stopped her from pacing back and forth.
"Take it easy. He's not as bad as you think he is."

Batting her eyes rapidly, she exclaimed, "How can anybody work with a man like that? What makes him think he can talk to me that way? Who does he think he is?"

"Hey, hey. Come on now. You can't let him get to you. It's your first day. Besides, I think you stung him in there. He didn't expect you to be so bold."

Symone raved on. "Well, he asked for it. Is he married? 'Cause if he is, I feel sorry for her," she continued. By the smile on Josiah's face, she guessed that her chattering was amusing him.

Josiah laughed. "Come on, now. You can't let him get to you," he said, holding her in his arms. "And he's not married."

"Thank God," she said, relieved. She was so agitated that she barely realized that he was holding her and she was holding him.

"He's uptight because the commissioner is on his back to wrap up this investigation ASAP."

For a second, Symone felt safe in Josiah's arms. Then, realizing that she was holding him too, she quickly pulled away.

Staring into Josiah's eyes, she was aware that she felt no friction or uneasiness toward him. He had proven to be a strong ally; she could afford to be comfortably herself with him. That was something she hadn't expected. "I'm sorry. I didn't mean to go off like that." She could see how baffled Josiah was from her sudden rebuff.

"No. I'm the one who's sorry," he said.

Symone tried to ignore her body's reaction to him; the racing heart, the tingling sensation down her spine and the strong urge to kiss him. She found Josiah to be irresistible. From the way he looked at her, it seemed he felt the same about her.

He opened the car door for her and Symone got in. He then walked around to his side of the car and got in. "Come on. I'll take you to the scene of the last murder." Starting the ignition and putting the car into gear, Josiah drove off the parking lot.

Seven

The chartered boat, putting incessantly, slowly made its way through the marshy waters of the steamy bayou.

Standing on the starboard bow of the Sea Urchin, Symone shooed at annoying flies and smacked away biting bugs as the captain of the small vessel steered through the Louisiana swamps.

The calling of wild birds and the slithering motions of an occasional alligator swimming through the muddy, mucky waters, added a certain "Tarzan of the Jungle" ambiance to their voyage. The strong whiff of marsh water along the dark river banks hung heavy in the air.

A sudden stench, intensified by the scorching southern Louisiana sun, impelled Symone to breathe through a handkerchief. The stench smelled like something had rotted. "We must be getting close," she said through the handkerchief.

Approaching Symone from the boat's helm, Josiah said, "If you think that's bad, you should have been here when we first started discovering bodies out here. This is mild compared to what this bayou used to smell like."

Witnessing another alligator submerging, Symone said, "I'm sure the gators weren't complaining. I'm just amazed anything was found out here at all, with these murky waters and hungry reptiles. Thank goodness for small miracles." She swatted another pesky mosquito.

"Well, the shallow water helped a bit. Thank God we didn't get heavy rains, or else we would never have found the bodies," he said.

Symone responded with a grunt.

As the boat bumped ashore, the captain cut the engine and turned to Josiah, who pulled out some money from his pocket. "Wait for us here. We'll be a few minutes," Josiah said. He slipped the captain a crisp twenty.

Symone stepped to the edge of the boat and looked down. She hesitated to get off because of the thick black mud at the river's edge.

Josiah joined her. "What's the matter?"

"If I had known you were going to hustle me out here on my first day, I would have dressed the part. I don't have on the right shoes." Josiah looked down at her feet. "These Easy Spirits aren't exactly mud-proof."

"Not a problem." Josiah hurtled over the side of the boat into the nasty sludge. He extended his arms toward Symone.

She looked down at him, standing in the black muck. "Now what?"

"Jump."

"Jump? You must be kidding, right?"

Nope. Jump. I'll catch you."

Symone took a step backward. "I think you better rethink this one, Agent La'Mon. If I jump and you slip—"

Josiah chuckled and clapped his hands at her. "Come on, don't be afraid. I'll catch you, I promise."

Laughing and taking another step backward, Symone said, "I think you better rethink that. If I jump and you slip with me in your arms—"

"I'm gonna catch you. C'mon, trust me." He motioned to her with his hands.

Reluctantly, Symone stepped toward the side of the boat and prepared to throw her leg over.

Then Josiah shouted, "Wait! How much do you weigh?"

A playful giggle escaped his mouth, evoking a snarl from Symone. She climbed over the side of the boat, jumped and landed in his arms.

With her arms tightly secured around his neck, and his strong, muscular arms wrapped around her waist, Symone and Josiah were as close as two strangers could get. His attractiveness was enticing. She realized how dangerous it was being this close to him. Their faces were so near that their noses touched.

They gazed into each other eyes, then Josiah hoisted her petite frame against his chest. He said in a low voice, "See? I kept my promise."

Swallowing the lump in her throat, she said, "So you did." She realized how safe she felt in his arms. She was aware, as well, how charming Josiah was. He was becoming more and more like her knight in shining armor, rather than her partner in crime.

"You know," Josiah said, still holding her in his arms, "since your arrival, it seems that you're always ending up in my arms. Should I be concerned?" His coy grin sent Symone's heart racing.

She batted her eyes like a child. "Not at all. Believe me when I say I'm not in your arms because I want to be. It's the shoes."

Josiah carried her over the wet mud to dry ground, where he let her down. "I wouldn't be too sure it's the shoes," he said, proceeding up the open path.

Symone gaped in surprise. "Excuse me?"

Treading up a grassy trail, Josiah yelled back, "Just watch your step. You might wind up stepping on a gator's tail."

Jerking her head downward, Symone made quick tracks of her own up the grassy hill behind Josiah.

When they arrived at the site of the last murder, the opening to the grave was still exposed. The police tape that had closed off the crime scene was now tattered and torn, flapping in the light afternoon breeze.

"How many people did you say were found here?" Symone stepped to the edge of the hole and looked down.

"Two," Josiah called back to her. He stood in a nearby thicket, scraping the mud from his shoes. "They were college students. We think they hitched a ride, not knowing it would be their last. They didn't make their destination, although some of their body parts did end up at one of the local post offices stamped 'Anywhere'. The awful smell coming from the package alerted the office supervisor. In turn, he called the police."

Symone cringed at the thought. "Were any fingerprints lifted from any of the crime scenes?"

"Not a one. But I'm more than confident that our killer will screw up sooner or later." Josiah walked over to Symone.

"Let's just hope sooner rather than later," she said as they both stepped away from the shallow hole in the ground.

After they had covered an hour's worth of ground, the hot sun and relentless humidity got to Symone. She felt woozy and stumbled.

Reaching out, Josiah grabbed her by the arm. "Are you all right?"

"Yeah. Boy, this heat ain't no joke," Symone said. She saw the concern on his face.

"I think we've been out here long enough. I'll take you back to the hotel."

Making their way back to the boat, Josiah took the opportunity to ask Symone some questions. "Can I ask you something?"

"Sure."

As they walked side by side down the path, the moss-heavy trees provided some welcome shade, and a nice breeze gave some momentary relief to the heat. "Mmm. That feels good," Symone said, fanning her face with her hand.

"Who did you have to leave behind to take this case?" Josiah asked, picking a leaf off a nearby tree.

Symone gave a shy grin. "I'm not sure I understand your question, Agent La'Mon."

"Wait a minute." Josiah reached out and stopped Symone in her stride. "We've already known each other for—" he glanced down at his gold Rolex, "—four hours, and you still insist on being formal. From now on, since we'll be working closely together, at least we should be comfortable enough to call each other by our first names."

"All right...Josiah."

"That's much better." They continued their walk down the grassy hill. "Now, you were saying?"

"I was about to say, the only thing I left behind was my cat, Sebastian. When my lieutenant informed me and my partner about the case, we had no choice."

"You could have said 'No'."

"Yeah, I could of. But why? This is what I do. This is my life. So, here I am."

Josiah turned and looked at her with a pleasant smile. "Are you always this easy? And I mean that in the most respectable way."

Symone laughed. The more they were together, the more she found herself enjoying being with him. "Of course. I treat people the way I want to be treated. Although that wasn't happening between me and your lieutenant."

They shared a chuckle.

"Like I said before," said Josiah, "you don't have to worry about DeClaud. As far as I'm concerned, to get to you, he would have to come through me. And for the record, no one has been able to do that yet."

Symone and Josiah shared a warm glance. "Well, now. That's good to know," she said.

When they got to the end of the path, where the grass and mud met, Symone stopped abruptly.

"Oh, yeah. I forgot," Josiah scooped up Symone into his arms. "I can learn to like this."

"Just don't like it too much. Sometimes I can be quite the handful," she said, staring into his big brown, slanted eyes.

Josiah pulled her close to his chest and said, "I'll take my chances."

He began his trek through the mud toward the boat. Just as he lifted her body up, his foot sank into a mud hole and down he went. Luckily, the captain caught Symone by the arms and pulled her safely aboard. Josiah wasn't so lucky. He landed butt first in the black, gooey muck. He was up to his elbows in filth.

On the boat, Symone and the captain snickered under their breaths.

❄ ❄ ❄

Back at the hotel, Josiah and Symone sat talking in the car.

"You're sure you don't want to come in?" Symone asked. "Surely housekeeping can find something to get that awful dirt out of your clothes."

Josiah looked down at the stains on his shirt, pants and shoes, as well as the mud on the steering wheel, the uphol-stery and carpet. "I don't believe there's anything strong enough on the market to get this mess out. I might as well throw everything in the trash. All because I was trying to be a gentleman."

"See? You're making me feel really bad. How was I to know that hole was there?"

"What was I supposed to do, drop you? I'm not that kind of guy. I'm a gentleman to the end."

"Well, in that case, there's no reason for you to decline my request, is there?" She flashed him an enchanting smile.

By a show of his pearly whites, Symone knew he would not refuse her. Besides, this was a good time to get to know her new partner better.

Josiah parked his car in the underground garage of the hotel, then accompanied Symone to her room, muddy clothes and all.

Eight

Once they entered her suite, Symone demanded that Josiah take off all his clothes, take a shower and put on the large terry cloth robe hanging behind the bathroom door.

After Symone called down to the front desk, room service came and retrieved his soiled cloths. Then she called for room service again and ordered dinner for both of them. She requested two filet mignons topped with crisped leeks and marsala reduction, served with fresh vegetables and wine. She got the waiter to slide a small table onto the balcony, where she dressed it with candles and fresh flowers, brought in earlier by the maid.

The scent of the succulent meal lured Josiah out of the bathroom. He seemed to have on nothing more than the oversized bathrobe, which perfectly fitted the contours of his hard, muscular body. He greeted Symone with a smile and bare feet.

Inhaling the aroma deeply, Josiah followed his nose to the balcony. "Wow. What smells so good?"

"Come and have a seat." She invited him to join her at the small, intimate table for two, beneath the Cajun moon. "I thought about how nice you've treated me my first day here and how you were always there to save the day. I wanted to show my appreciation and to say thank you." His big smile was an indication that he was pleased.

Dining among the stars, Symone and Josiah sat down to share a quiet meal and good conversation.

"What a way to end a day—good wine, good food, and good company," he said. He took one bite of the filet mignon. "Mmm. Delicious. Did you prepare all this while I was in the bathroom?" he joked. "In your little kitchenette?"

Laughing at his sense of humor, Symone blushed. "Are you kidding? I couldn't do all of this if someone paid me."

"I'm sure you can cook rings around those people downstairs. And it would probably taste better, too."

Symone was delighted that her day hadn't ended with paperwork, as it would have if she was back in Baltimore. Instead, she was having dinner with a man who had turned out to be nothing like she had expected. She had thought she would have to work with an arrogant, hard-nosed perfectionist, who had all the answers but couldn't care less about the questions. To her surprise, Josiah had turned out to be the opposite. He was funny, caring and, most of all, he knew his job. Maybe that was the attraction she felt, she thought to herself.

She looked at him from across the table and smiled. "You know, I have to be honest with you."

Josiah picked up his glass of red wine and sipped. "About what?"

"I didn't exactly believe we would get along. You're not exactly what I expected. I was wrong about you. I don't say that too often."

"If it'll make you feel any better, you're not exactly what I expected, either."

Symone's eyes widened in surprise. "Oh, really? What exactly did you expect?"

He teased her by pretending to avoid her question. "Ump. Did you taste the leeks? They're delicious."

"Don't play." Symone tossed her napkin across the table at him. "What did you mean by that remark?"

Josiah laughed. "I was kidding. You're exactly what I expected—and more."

Their eyes met. A warm fuzzy feeling settled in her belly.

"You're dedicated, unrelenting, and good at what you do. Any agent would be proud to have you cover his ass." With a sly glance he added, "But..."

"But what?"

His gaze rested upon her face. "You're much prettier in person."

Symone lowered her eyes to shield herself from his sultry gaze and to hide her own emotions. "Considering how we first met, and how things are still unfolding, I'm flattered by your words."

He leaned back in his chair; the top of the robe opened slightly, exposing the black curly locks of his chest hairs. It was hard for Symone to look away. She was drawn to her new partner like a flame to a wick. "I'm glad that you're flattered. I meant every word," he said.

A warm, tingling sensation settled between her thighs as his words dripped from his lips like sweet honey.

Symone reminded herself that she had to stay focused on the case. She was letting her thoughts run wild in her head. She attempted to change the subject. "So, what conclusions have you come up with about this case?" She saw the slow change on his face, and knew he didn't want to use this time talking shop.

Josiah sighed. "There are still some things that don't quite mesh." The expression on his face was serious; and Symone could tell that the case was taking its toll on him. "For the life of me, I still can't help but feel we're overlooking something."

"Like what?" Symone raked her finger across the white whipped cream of the strawberry shortcake, which was dessert.

"Well, remember earlier I said that it's like the killer is always two steps ahead of us?"

Symone nodded her head.

"Well, whenever it seems like we're falling behind, it's almost like he waits, giving us time to catch up."

"That's not very smart."

"That's not how the killer would see it. From the very beginning, he has carefully choreographed this dance with death. He's set the stage, not for himself, but for us," he said, sipping his wine.

"I don't quite get it."

"Killing is a game to him," he continued. "And we're part of the game. He wants us to pay attention."

Slapping her hand on the table, she said, "Well, hell, he's got my attention."

"I know it sounds crazy. I figure it like this. For a long time, he got away with everything and never got caught. In his head, he's created this indestructible character who, he believes, can't be stopped. But, he's in for a rude awakening."

Josiah seemed to be getting too serious, so Symone changed the subject again to lighten the mood. "How about a piece of this sinful-looking cake?"

Smiling, Josiah rubbed his stomach. "I don't know if I have room for it. I've never had room service this good before." His voice was low and sexy.

She found his sensuality overpowering and hard to handle. "Tell me something, Josiah—and please don't take this the wrong way. But what are you?"

He choked on his wine. "Excuse me?" he asked, wiping his mouth with the napkin.

"I don't mean what are you exactly, but what nationality are you? Every now and again, I detect an accent. And your eyes—they look almost Oriental."

"I'm African-American mixed with Cajun and Japanese."

"That's a whole lot of people inside one person. Your bio didn't mention that."

"Should it have?"

"No, but—"

"I know. You were just curious, right?"

"You could say that. I hope I didn't offend you?"

"No, you didn't. When I first started this career, I got the same sorts of questions and weird stares. So, no. It doesn't bother me. In fact, I like to keep people guessing."

"Are there any more La'Mons around and about?"

"Mmm. My folks here in New Orleans. And I have three sisters up in Detroit."

It seemed whenever the words between them were few, Symone found the silence unbearable. The sexual chemistry between her and Josiah was more than she had expected. Symone found herself feeling like a shy schoolgirl around him.

"Well. No use in sitting here." He rose from his chair. "I can at least clear the table for you." He reached over, picked up her plate and silverware, and placed it back onto the kitchen cart in the corner of the balcony.

"Thank you." Symone was enjoying having him there with her.

As Josiah busied himself with the dishes, Symone took the opportunity to really appreciate his manliness. Every time he came near her, she took in a good whiff of the fresh, clean scent he left behind as he moved about.

"Maybe I should call down to check on your clothes," she said.

"What's the rush? Why don't you go inside and relax on the sofa while I finish up here?"

Symone got up and walked inside.

After he had cleared the table, Josiah joined her in the living room. As he sat down beside her, Symone rubbed the back of her neck.

"What's wrong?" Josiah asked.

"I guess I'm just tired. It has been a long day. But don't worry, I'll be fine."

With a gesture that seemed natural, Josiah reached over and gently squeezed the back of her neck. "You're tight." He got up and walked behind the sofa. He placed his large hands at Symone's neck.

Instinctively, Symone jerked away from his touch. "You really don't have to do—" The gentle kneading stopped Symone in mid-sentence. She moaned; her eyes slowly closed as he applied pressure to her tight, over-worked muscles.

"Ooo...Mmmm...Ahhh. Right there."

"Right there?" Josiah responded in a low voice.

Symone felt herself surrendering to his will. Soon her entire body went limp.

Josiah did with his hands what no professional masseuse could do for her. His fingers awakened sensations in her she hadn't realized she had. It was as if he were caressing her right down to her soul. Josiah had her purring like a kitten.

"How does that feel?"

Her chin slowly bowed to her chest. "Mmm...Good."

His hands made their way across her shoulder blades, down the sides of her arms and up again to her shoulders.

"Yes! Yes! Right there. Don't stop," she exclaimed.

Josiah lowered his face to her ear and whispered, "I won't."

By this time, Symone was doubled-over from sheer relaxation. Josiah carefully and consistently raked up and down her spine with his fingertips. Symone arched her back like a lazy cat as each stimulating stroke heated her skin. She was really feeling— the tantalizing sensation that erupted in the pit of her belly, and flowed downward between her thighs.

Suddenly Josiah stopped. "Come with me." He walked around the sofa, took Symone by the hands and pulled her to her feet.

A bit disoriented, she pulled back. "What? What's the matter?"

Her stomach muscles suddenly tightened as he held her close to his thick chest. "Just keep walking." He turned and tugged her along like a child. When Symone saw that he was leading her in the direction of the bedroom, she began to drag her feet.

"I don't think going in there is such a good idea, Josiah. Really."

"Ssh. I want you to lie down. You'll really get more of the effect of the massage if you're totally relaxed and comfortable."

They crossed the threshold of the bedroom and Josiah lowered Symone's body to the bed.

Her voice quivered. "Shouldn't I be lying on my stomach?"

"First, let's get this shirt off." Symone's gaze never left his. Her body trembled involuntarily as his hands went to the first button of her silk blouse. The excitement and fear she felt was quickly consuming her. Her heart pounded wildly in her chest as his fingers tenderly glided across her breast.

When the last button was undone, Josiah slowly opened her blouse, exposing her soft, brown breasts, which spilled out of the seafoam-colored bra she wore.

Just as Josiah was casually running his hand down the middle of her breast, he was rudely interrupted by a knock at the door.

"Front desk," a voice bellowed outside the door.

Symone abruptly jumped off the bed and raced to the door, buttoning her blouse at the same time. She opened the door with such urgency that she startled the bellman.

The young man handed her Josiah's clothes wrapped in brown tissue paper. "Thank you so very much," she said in relief. His timing couldn't have been more perfect. She gave him a five-dollar tip.

Josiah walked out of the bedroom. "I take it those are my clothes, right?"

Symone turned in his direction. He stood with his arms folded against his chest. "All pressed and ready to wear." She extended the package to him.

Josiah looked at her with a crooked grin. "I guess this is my cue, huh?"

Symone stood in the middle of room, breathing a sigh of relief. "I believe so."

Josiah took the bag into the bathroom to dress. Symone dropped to the sofa, wiping imaginary sweat from her brow. "That was close," she mumbled.

Josiah walked out of the bathroom carrying the robe in his hand. Symone sprang from the sofa and the two stood before each other without a word.

"Until tomorrow, then." He handed her the robe.

Symone walked him to the door. As she watched him standing there in the doorway, Symone's body tingled. "Good night, Josiah."

He reached out and stroked her cheek. "Good night, Symone." He turned and walked toward the elevator. Symone closed and locked the door behind him. With her back to the door, she exhaled.

That was a close one, she thought. After losing Jordan, she wasn't sure she was ready to love again. At least not yet.

But what a temptation Josiah La'Mon was.

Nine

Early the next morning, the ringing of the phone awakened Symone from her sleep. She answered in a groggy voice. "Hello."

"Detective Rawlins." The tone of the man's voice was brash and commanding. "DeClaud here. It's imperative that you get to the station ASAP! Agent La'Mon is on his way to pick you up." The call abruptly ended without Symone having a chance to respond.

She glanced at the clock on the night stand; it was 6:00 in the morning.

When Symone reached the lobby, she saw that Josiah was already waiting outside in the car. She got in. "What's the emergency?"

Josiah skidded off as Symone's butt hit the finely crafted leather seats. He flew down the semi-deserted streets like a bat out of hell. "We just got a tip that our suspect is hiding out at a motel downtown."

When they arrived at the precinct, chaos had already spread. Plainclothes and uniformed officers charged to their vehicles, as sirens rang out. A large black truck with the initials S.W.A.T. pulled up, loaded down with armored men toting automatic assault weapons. Josiah guided Symone through the pandemonium. He stopped an officer as they were entering. "Where's the lieutenant?"

"He's already gone. He said to meet him there."

Running behind everyone else, Symone and Josiah raced to his car and peeled out of the police parking lot.

White, blue and red lights flashed, and sirens pierced the dead silence as the sun gradually peeked through a clear sky. Police vehicles stormed the intersections of downtown New Orleans, enroute to catch a killer.

The tension was mounting. The twenty-five-minute ride seemed like hours to Symone as she sat clutching the car handle above her head. Conversing over his car phone, Josiah tried to contact Lieutenant DeClaud. "Get me the lieutenant."

Waiting to get linked up to DeClaud, Josiah glanced at a worried Symone. "Are you ready for this, Detective?"

"As ready as I'll ever be."

Sharply taking a corner like a madman, Josiah said, "Don't worry. I won't let anything happen to you."

Symone turned in his direction. "I didn't come all this way for nothing."

Josiah swerved his car around a city block. The blaring, ear-piercing sound of his siren stopped vehicles and pedestrians in their tracks. Symone suspected the screeching noise could be heard several blocks away.

"Just so you know," he said, "I'll see that nothing happens to you."

"Don't worry about me. Just watch your own ass out there."

When they finally arrived at the location, it was like a scene from a movie. Cops were jumping out of their patrol cars, crouching down beside the car doors, using them as shields. Sharpshooters from the S.W.A.T. team leaped from the rear of the armored black truck, ran and perched on nearby rooftops to get a clear shot of the suspect.

Symone and Josiah darted to the front of the brigade, where they found DeClaud giving orders.

"I'll take over from here, Lieutenant." Josiah instructed.

"What took you guys so long?" DeClaud said, looking at them with an accusatory stare.

"You didn't exactly wait for us, Lieutenant," Symone said, crouching in close to Josiah.

"Don't worry, the party hasn't started yet." DeClaud smirked at Symone. "Get the sleep out of your eyes, Detective." His dry humor had no effect on Symone, who kept her eyes on Josiah.

She pulled her weapon from her back holster.

With walkie-talkie in hand, Josiah began to disperse the troops. "There will not be an exchange of gunfire until I say so. If we're lucky, we can pull this bastard out alive. Everybody got that?" His command was received loud and clear.

Symone observed her partner moving quietly and intently on the field. He had become more and more intriguing with each passing hour. If he was as good as she had heard, Symone knew she could look forward to a speedy return to Maryland. She eagerly anticipated a quick arrest, and hoped to be on the next flight out.

"Lieutenant," Josiah turned to DeClaud. "Detective Rawlins and I will make our way through the back entrance, while you send some of the other officers through the front."

Overwhelmed with sudden nostalgia, Symone thought of Jordan.

She remembered giving that same directive to her brother before he was killed.

"Detective. Are you with us?" DeClaud's cantankerous disposition jetted Symone back to reality. "If you're having second thoughts, Detective..."

"No, sir." She quickly followed behind Josiah as they made their move toward the motel.

One by one, two by two and four by four, the officers ran and took their positions. The sharpshooters aimed their rifles at the front door of the rundown motel, while others hid in doorways in nearby buildings across the street.

The intense heat from the morning sun began its assault on those below, as it rose high above the city.

In minutes, the building was surrounded by cops. Intrigued spectators gathered at the windows of a local McDonald's restaurant. They had a front row seat to all the action going down.

Inside the motel, Symone and Josiah made their way up the back stairs. As they ascended the concrete steps, their footsteps were halted when they heard DeClaud's southern drawl, echoing through a bullhorn. "This is NOPD. We have you surrounded. Come out with your hands up."

"What in the hell is he doing?" Josiah said angrily.

Symone shook her head in disbelief. DeClaud's actions were totally absurd. "Has he ever heard of the phrase 'the element of surprise'?" They could hear the crash of doors below, and the thunder of footsteps as the police stormed the building.

As Symone and Josiah entered through a door on the fifth floor, Symone said, "It's like finding a needle in a haystack." She followed behind Josiah down the dimly lit corridor.

With guns drawn, she and Josiah walked cautiously down the hall, expecting anything to happen. Josiah moved a few feet ahead of Symone; she covered his back, glancing over her shoulder every few seconds.

"How does DeClaud expect us to find one man with so many freaking doors he could be hiding behind?" she said.

"By now, the suspect has received our calling card."

As they passed one door, they heard the sounds of breaking glass behind a closed door down the hall. They approached room 503 and stood on opposite sides of the door.

Careful to keep clear, Josiah knocked on the door with the back of his hand, firmly gripping his pistol. "FBI and NOPD. Open up!"

The sound of fumbling and something hard hitting the floor inside the room prompted Symone and Josiah to prepare to enter. Josiah motioned to Symone to enter at the count of three. He silently counted down. At the count of three the two kicked in the door.

The door flew open and the doorknob crashed against the wall as it flung back with force. To their surprise, they had entered an empty room. The suspect had escaped.

The room was in shambles. The walls were covered with newspaper clippings, pictures, and other evidence pertaining to the murders.

Symone checked the room, careful not to disturb anything. Josiah made his way around the unmade bed and found a McDonald's breakfast, still warm, lying in the middle of the bed along with other newspaper clippings, shells from sunflower seeds, soiled sheets and an open telephone book. Empty soda and beer cans were littered on the floor, along with paper, chips and other filth.

"Where did he go that fast?" Josiah was befuddled.

Symone immediately called on the two-way radio. "Did anyone see anything? He got away. I repeat, he got away."

Soon, the voice of DeClaud invaded the airways. "Goddammit. Find him!"

"Son of a bitch," Josiah cursed.

"It looks as if he went by the window," Symone said, stepping around broken glass. She looked down to the street, past the fire escape. There was no sign of anyone. "The question is, how did he get by without someone seeing him? There are sharpshooters everywhere."

Josiah made his way to the open closet. He looked at the wall and saw the laundry chute. "Here's how he got away. He probably broke out the window to throw us off."

Symone moved over to the closet to see what Josiah was referring to. "The laundry chute?"

"Yep." He opened the chute door and stuck his arm in to see if he could feel anything.

"What is he? A contortionist or something?" Symone said.

"This chute is wide enough for a very lean person to slide through. We can rule out the window," he said, closing the hatch.

Lieutenant DeClaud finally caught up with them in the room. "Another dead end?" he commented sarcastically. "Well, what did we learn today, boys and girls? That the killer outsmarted us again."

"Yes, he did, thanks to your announcing our arrival," Josiah snapped back. "On whose authority are you operating, Lieutenant? Because you're obviously not taking my authority seriously."

"I just thought—"

Josiah stood in DeClaud's face. "I shouldn't have to remind you who's in charge here, Lieutenant. If you have a problem with that, I suggest you take it up with your superiors. Or else I will be forced to relieve you of your duties on this investigation. Do you understand?"

Symone looked over Josiah's shoulder at DeClaud's sudden red face. She could tell that DeClaud did not take Josiah's reprimand well. She stepped toward the two men. "Hey, look. We had him cornered. It's just a matter of time, right?" Josiah and DeClaud were at each other's throats. She didn't want their confrontation to turn into blows.

"Get Forensics up here now. I want this room swept," Josiah commanded an officer who had walked into the room.

Josiah walked over to the bed and picked up the opened telephone book. "What? Was he about to order pizza?"

Symone stepped to Josiah's side. The telephone book was opened to a list of cemeteries. "Obviously, there was a reason he looked this up."

"Obviously." Josiah ripped out the page.

"You're tampering with the evidence, Agent La'Mon," DeClaud said stiffly.

"Arrest me." Josiah took the sheet and he and Symone moved toward the door.

Before they could leave, the empty room was flooded with individuals in rubber gloves who would more than likely dust everything from the doorknob to the flush handle on the toilet.

Down in the lobby, Symone and Josiah stopped at the front desk.

"Is it me, or does he always seem to have a chip on his shoulder?" Symone asked.

"Oomph. I stopped worrying about his bad attitude a long time ago," Josiah responded. He took the telephone book page from his pocket and carefully ripped it in half. "He's just bitter because I moved in on his territory. That's what that's about. His ego is bruised because I'm in charge and he's not."

"You two are not bonding at all."

Josiah grunted. "Here." He gave Symone one half of the page and kept the other half. "We'll cover more ground if we split up. You go and check out the cemeteries on your half."

"Why do you think he had the book opened to cemeteries?"

"Either he's looking for a plot for himself, or he's leading us to his next victim." Josiah pulled a pen from his breast pocket. He drew a circle around a name on his half of the sheet. "We'll meet at the Lafayette Cemetery in three hours."

Two young people, a man and a woman, came up from behind the front desk. "Is it safe to come out now?" one of them asked in a quivering voice.

"Yeah." Josiah turned and looked at the front door hanging off its hinges. "Sorry about the door. You can send the bill to NOPD," he said with a mocking laugh.

The two young people looked as though they hardly found their present situation humorous.

"Can I ask you something? Who rented out room 503?" Symone inquired.

The young woman pulled up the computer screen and began to search. "The room was reserved by someone named K. Stokes. That's all it says."

Symone gasped.

"What's the matter?" Josiah said, turning towards her.

"That name. I know that name."

"K. Stokes?" he asked.

"Yes, K. Stokes. That was Johnny Blade's name. His real name was Kevin Stokes."

Josiah turned to the two people behind the desk. "Could you describe the person who rented that room?"

The young woman and man shrugged their shoulders with uncertainty.

Josiah frowned. "Symone, are you sure?"

"Positive."

"Could Johnny Blade have a brother?" he asked.

"It all makes sense now," she said, wide eyes.

"What are you talking about, Symone?"

"We'll find out soon enough." Symone pulled out her cellphone. She dialed her lieutenant back in Baltimore.

While Symone waited for Spaulding to come to the phone, Josiah pointed to a camera in the corner above the lobby counter. "Does that camera work?"

The two young people looked at each other suspiciously. Josiah, looked at them in the same way. "It either works or it doesn't. Which is it?"

The young man spoke first. "Well, sir. The manager likes for us to tell the customers it doesn't work."

"Why?" he asked.

The two clerks looked at each other again. "Well, because some of the clients that frequent here aren't just johns and prostitutes. Sometimes we get prominent people who come in. You know," he said, slyly, "people who wouldn't be too happy if they found themselves on videotape. If you know what I mean, sir."

Josiah nodded his head. "Yeah. I know what you mean. Tell me something. Just for the sake of asking, who exactly wouldn't want to find themselves on that tape?"

It was clear that neither of the clerks wanted to spill their guts. They repeatedly nudged each other in side, one wanting the other to tell.

"I promise you won't get in any trouble for telling me. I just want a name."

"Just one name?" the young woman said.

Josiah gave her a reassuring grin. "Just one."

"Okay. Just one. The mayor," she said quickly.

Josiah held in his grin at the thought of the mayor bringing someone other than his wife to a place like this. The motel wasn't exactly a five-star establishment. It wasn't exactly in the New Orleans travel brochure. "Is it possible that I can get a look at the footage that's been shot, say, for the last two weeks?"

"You would have to ask the manager, but he's on vacation."

"Well, who is in charge here?" Josiah asked.

"Holtz. The assistant manager, and he won't be in until tonight."

Pulling his business card from his pocket, Josiah turned the card over and wrote Symone's name and number on it. He handed the card to the clerk. "See that he calls either me, or the name on the back as soon as he gets in. It's very urgent that we see who's on that tape. Tell him it's a matter of life and death. Possibly his own, if the killer comes back," Josiah warned.

Symone had a few words with her lieutenant on the phone, then ended her conversation and walked up to Josiah.

"Well, what did he say?" Josiah asked.

"He said he'll run a background check for me. It'll take at least two days before we know anything."

Josiah looked at her intently. "Let's hope two days is all we need."

The two left the motel and headed for the cemeteries.

Ten

The Lafayette Cemetery was one of oldest cemeteries in the city, a virtual maze of above-ground crypts. Because New Orleans is below sea level, the high water table prevents interments in the ground.

After checking half a dozen cemeteries, Symone finally caught up with Josiah at the iron-gated entrance to Lafayette.

"There you are." Josiah came out from behind one of the tombs just inside the gate.

"I don't think we're in Kansas anymore, Toto," she joked. To her surprise, the entire cemetery had an enchanted allure to it, something Symone had expected to find only in a book of fairytales. "So, what are we looking for?" she asked.

"Can I help you folks?" A voice from behind startled them.

Out of the shadows between two crypts appeared an elderly man, tall and lanky in stature. In his hand he carried a hoe and shovel. He greeted them with a friendly smile, which exposed several missing teeth. He had a severe case of sunburn on his face and neck.

"How can I help y'all good folks?" The old man reached into the pocket of his jumpsuit, pulled out a dingy handkerchief and wiped his sweaty face.

Symone and Josiah showed him their badges. "Are you in charge here?" Josiah asked.

"I'm just the groundskeeper. Is something wrong?"

"We were hoping you could tell us," Symone interjected. "Have you had any trouble around here, say, in the last couple of days?"

"Trouble? Naw. No trouble here."

"What about anything suspicious or strange? Maybe you've seen or heard something out of the ordinary," Josiah said.

The man coughed up brown phlegm and spat on the ground. The gross brownish-yellow stains on his teeth were a telltale sign that he smoked a lot, aside from the hoarse cough that interrupted him when he spoke. Symone felt a slight queasiness every time he spat.

"I've been carin' for dese grounds since the last war, and I ain't seen nuthin' out here, 'cept stuff dese crazy kids ha'done."

"Like what?" Symone asked. Looking at the state some of the tombs were in, she wondered what 'carin' for dese grounds' actually meant.

"Ya know, bustin' into some graves, stealin' jewelry off da dead, bashing tombstones. Ya know, the usual."

"Other than that, that's all?" Josiah stared at the old man.

"Well...y'all come with me."

Treading through the maze of stone edifices, he led Symone and Josiah to a marble crypt that was the size of a small cabin. It was set apart from all the other mausoleums in the cemetery. As they approached the tomb, Symone could see that the door to the crypt had been forced open and was barely hanging on to its hinges.

"Somebody desecrated this beautiful home of the dead," the old-timer said regretfully.

"Do you know why someone would do this?" Symone inquired.

Josiah pushed the door open the rest of the way.

The old-timer scratched his head. "Why do evil folk do anythin', is what I'd like to know. I suppose they can't afford sumum' this fancy."

Josiah stepped inside the semi-dark crypt. He turned to Symone. "You got a lighter?"

"No. Would you happen to have a flashlight, sir?" she asked the old man.

"I could getcha' one. It's jus' up yonder in my pickup. I'll go fetch it for ya." The old man darted out of the tomb faster than a jackrabbit.

Symone chuckled. "I get the feeling being inside one of these things is not where he wants to be."

"Do you blame him? " Josiah responded as he looked around the dark, dank mausoleum.

"Get a load of this." Symone peered into the gloom. There was enough light to see clippings taped to the walls of the tomb. She squinted at the walls, and saw that they were clippings related to the murders. There was even an old newspaper clipping with her in it, which had been taken during Blade's reign of terror in Maryland. Symone's picture had a big, red "X" on it. An eerie chill slithered down her spine as she ripped the article off the wall. "I guess it's safe to say that the killer knows who I am and why I'm here."

Josiah stood at her side. He gently placed his hand on hers to console her. "He may know who you are, but he doesn't know where you are. There's a difference."

"Not too much, though. Does this mean he'll be coming after me next?" Symone turned to him in the darkness.

"Not if I can help it." The two shared a moment of silence. "What's taking that old man so long?" Josiah stepped toward the open door and peered out impatiently. "He probably got lost himself. Will you be all right? I'm

Charlene A. Berry

gonna go to the car. I think I may have a flashlight in the trunk"

Symone gave him a grin. "Sure. Go ahead."

"I won't be but a minute." Josiah hastened out of the tomb toward his car.

Symone stood at the mouth of the crypt; the still, creepy place made her feel on edge. She patted herself down; she recalled having a book of matches somewhere on her. She rummaged in her blazer pocket and found the book.

Striking the match lit up the gloomy crypt momentarily. "Then there was light," she said in a mocking voice. The small flame barely did the job, but it was enough for her to notice a dark mass lying in one of the corners of the tomb. Symone walked over and knelt in front of it. Her back was toward the entrance as she started to grab the object; then the match burned down to her finger. "Ouch!" she cried. She struck another match. When there was light again, she carefully unwrapped what turned out to be a cloth pouch tied together with a string. As the contents hit the concrete floor, the familiar clang of a knife sounded in her ears.

"Well, well, well. What do we have here?" Using the cloth, Symone picked up the knife. She attempted to examine it by the small, flickering light, but found it difficult to do. The match once again burned out. She struck another one.

"Could this be the weapon used to kill his victims?" She held the flame up to the sharp grooves of the knife. There was dried blood within the jagged notches. By the light of the flame, Symone found more evidence—a pair of bloody gloves, some twine, and duct tape.

As footsteps approached her from behind, she said, "You won't believe what I just found, Josiah." When she didn't get a response, she started to turn. The door to the tomb suddenly slammed shut, and she was engulfed in darkness.

"What the hell!" She felt herself ambushed from behind. Struggling with her assailant, she was placed in a choke hold. A petrifying sense of urgency gripped her heart when the attacker wrapped his strong arms around her neck, obstructing her air supply. Symone felt as though the blood vessels in her head were about to burst.

Fiercely she attempted to fight him off, but to no avail. He clearly had Symone right where he wanted her. Back and forth in darkness they tussled. She wanted to scream, but she knew her screams would be muffled by the thick walls of the tomb. She lifted her foot, kicked her attacker on the leg with the heel of her shoe. She followed with a quick blow to his face with her elbow. Symone was now free to grab her weapon and fall to the floor, but she didn't fire for fear the ricocheting bullets would hit her. "I've got a gun!" she yelled into the darkness.

Suddenly, the door to the tomb swung open. Adjusting her eyes to the bright sunlight, Symone ran in pursuit. She commenced to fire numerous times at a suspect who was faster than she was. However, she had gotten a brief look at her assailant when he ran out the door. He was of medium build and had on dark clothing. She couldn't get a clear look at his face because his back was toward her, but she saw that he wore some sort of dark, hooded shirt. That was all she could make out.

She yelled out, "Stop. Police!"

She ran through the maze of tombs, turning to follow the man as he darted in and out between them. She fired one shot at him just before she tripped and fell to the ground. When she looked up, the suspect had disappeared somewhere in the labyrinth of crypts.

Doubled over and cradling her wounded knee, Symone panted wildly and wheezed as if her lungs were about to burst.

Suddenly, the sound of running footsteps came from behind her. Symone quickly picked up her gun, prepared to shoot. She turned and saw Josiah charging toward her with his gun drawn. As he drew closer, she saw the dread on his face.

"Symone! Are you all right?" He hurried to her side.

"Where were you?" she asked angrily.

Bending down beside her and breathing erratically, Josiah attempted to touch her leg. She slapped his hand away.

"What do you mean? I went back to the tomb, and you weren't there." he said. "I heard the shot and I came running."

"I was almost killed. Somebody attacked me after you left. I found something in the tomb, and when I was about to turn around, the killer grabbed me from behind and tried to strangle me."

"When I heard the gunshot, I came running as fast I could."

"Well, obviously your definition of fast wasn't fast enough!" she said with outrage in her voice. "He got away."

Josiah looked taken aback by her attitude. "Well, I'm sorry that my best isn't good enough for you, Detective." His hard gaze fell upon her face. "Next time, I'll think twice before leaving you alone, seeing you can't handle yourself."

Josiah's sharp remark surprised Symone. She considered her own heated words, which she had flung at him. "I'm sorry," she said. "I didn't mean to come off at you like that. It's just that I've been close to death before, but this was too damn close for comfort."

Josiah stood up and extended his hand to her again. "Will you let me help you?"

Symone looked up at him and finally gave him her hand.

"Now, if we're going to solve this case together, you gotta learn to trust me, Symone. Or do I have to solve this case alone?"

She gripped his hand and rose to her feet. "In case you didn't know, I'm not a quitter. No matter what happens, we're in this thing together. Even if we have to chase that S.O.B. into the next millennium."

Josiah pulled her limp body to his chest. "Well, let's hope we catch him before then." He glanced down at her ripped pants. Her knee was bleeding. When she fell, she cut it on the granite plot marker that she had tripped over. "You'll live. But you're gonna have one nasty scar. You think you can walk?"

"I think so." Symone leaned her weight on her leg but it immediately buckled under the pressure.

"Never mind." Josiah swooped her up in his arms and carried her out of the cemetery.

Discreetly, she examined his profile. Once again, he was there to save the day—well, more or less. She could get used to this, she thought, as he carried her to safety.

When they emerged from the tombs, they were greeted at the gate to the cemetery by blaring sirens, flashing lights, and Lieutenant DeClaud.

"When I heard the call that two of my officers were under attack, I brought the cavalry." His gaze fell upon Symone in Josiah's arms. "What happened to you?"

"It's just a little cut. I'm fine."

His expression told Symone that he didn't believe her. "Agent La'Mon, would you care to explain?"

"One minute I was at the car getting a flashlight out of the trunk, and the next minute I heard a gunshot. I go running through the cemetery and find Detective Rawlins on the ground in pain."

"I'm fine," said Symone. "In fact, you can put me down."

Josiah ignored her request. DeClaud whistled for a paramedic from a waiting ambulance which had been called to the scene.

"Lieutenant, I don't need to go to the hospital. I'm all right," she said to DeClaud.

"Look. The paramedics are here. Let them take a look at you."

"Okay, if it'll make you both happy, I'll let them check me out."

"And after that, I'm taking you back to the hotel. You had enough for the day," Josiah said.

"But—" Symone attempted to interject.

Josiah forestalled her by saying, "Aaat. I don't want to hear it."

"Lieutenant," Symone started to say.

DeClaud just shook his head and walked away.

Symone gave Josiah a stern look as he set her down in the back of the ambulance. After the medics had cleaned and dressed the wound, and given her an ice pack to keep the swelling down, Josiah helped her into his car and they left the scene. DeClaud stayed behind to gather the evidence.

Eleven

Symone lay in her hotel bed with the ice bag on her knee, which was propped on two pillows. Josiah was in the kitchen, fixing her a cup of tea.

"Can you hear me?" Symone yelled from the bed.

"Yeah. What did you say?" he yelled back from the kitchen.

"I said, did you call for backup out there?"

Josiah returned to the bedroom carrying a tray with a steaming cup of tea on it.

"I heard you the first time. No. I didn't call. There was no time. When I heard the shot, I came running."

"Well, how did the lieutenant find out? You think the old man called the police?"

"Possible. I mean, who else could it have been? He sure stayed out of sight when the police finally did arrive."

"I guess the poor old geezer was scared out of his mind."

Josiah sat beside her on the side of the bed. "Here you go, some nice mint tea." He put the cup gently to her lips. Symone sipped.

"Ooh. It's hot, but good." He placed the cup in the saucer. She didn't know what was more soothing—the warmth of the tea gliding down her throat, or the warmth of Josiah's affection. She felt ridiculous just lying here like an invalid; so she started to get up off the bed.

"Uh, where do you think you're going?" Josiah gently placed his hand on her shoulder to stop her.

"To the bathroom. I want to take a shower. Do you mind?" she said with a stubborn edge in her voice.

"As a matter of fact, I do. You lie still and I'll go draw you a bath."

He left Symone's side and went into the bathroom. Symone couldn't help but be tickled by his authoritative conduct, even off duty.

The sound of rushing water and the mild fragrance of peach nectar floated from the bathroom into the bedroom.

Returning with his shirtsleeves rolled to his elbows, Josiah stood at the foot of the bed.

She smiled graciously at him. "You really do know how to spoil a girl."

Josiah approached the side of the bed where she lay. "My mother didn't raise just a boy. She raised a gentleman." He scooped Symone off the bed and into his arms.

She wrapped her arm around his neck. "Be careful. I could get used to this."

As he walked toward the bathroom, she noticed his uneven stride. "Are you limping?"

Josiah seemed to brush off her concern. "It's nothing. It's just a light sprain I got coming to your rescue."

"Maybe I should be carrying you," Symone joked, tightening her embrace around his neck. She stared at him intently as he carried her. She thought how easy it would be to fall in love with him. He was everything she had ever dreamed of in a man. He was kind, caring and very protective of her. Why couldn't she fall in love with him? Maybe, she thought with a sigh, he would have to feel the same way about her. Only then could she trust her heart.

She laid her head on his shoulder. "Why is it that you're always managing to save me?"

He walked into the bathroom and let her down gently on the rug, still holding her close to his chest. "Maybe because I want to," he responded in a seductive voice.

Their faces were so close that Symone could feel his hot breath on her lips. Her body began to tingle all over. "Aren't I the lucky one."

As their noses briefly touched, Josiah whispered, "My sentiments exactly."

He reached past her and turned off the water in the tub. He tested it by sticking his hand beneath the frothy pink foam. The playful bubbles filled the octagon-shaped tub, as the jets from the whirlpool stirred the water. "In the words of Goldilocks, 'It's just right.'"

Symone hobbled to the tub and dipped her hand in the water. "Mmm. I think you're right," she responded, looking up at him. "Okay. Turn your back," she commanded. For a second, Josiah didn't move. Symone forced him around by grabbing his arms and twisting his body toward the wall. She used his back and shoulders as a crutch to hold on to as she undressed.

She suddenly felt deliciously wicked. She pulled off her shirt and tossed it at Josiah's feet. She then pulled off her bra and draped it across his shoulder. She unbuttoned her pants; they too were deposited at his feet. When she pulled off her panties and tossed them at Josiah's feet, she could imagine his eyes raising toward the ceiling.

She stepped into the tub, wincing as the soap hit her scraped knee, then relaxed as the pain passed. As her body sank beneath a blanket of delicate, creamy bubbles, Symone playfully cleared her throat. "You can turn around now."

He turned slowly. Her face was the only thing not covered by foam. His steps were awkward. "Maybe I should leave." As he backed toward the door, Symone beckoned to him.

"No, please stay." She glanced over her shoulder at him. "I may need help getting at those hard to reach spots."

He pulled a towel from the rack and folded it several times until it was firm. He then placed the towel behind Symone's head.

"Thank you, Josiah."

He seemed to be trying desperately not to look upon her nakedness.

Symone reached up and took the sponge. She dipped it in the water. "Could you help me?" She was purposely pushing his buttons. She knew that he was a strong man physically. But she wanted to know just how strong he really was, when it came to matters of the heart.

Josiah knelt down beside the tub. She handed him the sponge and he took it. She laid her head back on the towel and extended her arm to him. Josiah took her arm into his hand and gently wiped up and down.

As he followed the sponge with his hand, stroking a trail of pink foam across her shoulders and chest, Symone sank deeper into the water. Closing her eyes, she let out a small whimper that escaped from her damp, slightly parted lips. Josiah carefully dipped the sponge back into the water. Symone gradually allowed her brown breasts to peek through the soft, wet bubbles. Josiah cautiously diverted his hands elsewhere, but Symone boldly guided him back. She allowed him to touch the forbidden places he would otherwise not have ventured to touch on his own.

The perspiration glistened on their faces as the temperature in the room began to rise, partly from the steaming bath, partly from their own heat. Symone continued to let him explore her under the water, without the sponge. She moaned and sighed breathlessly as he delved deep between her thighs with one hand, while he teased her nipples with the other.

Symone was finally allowing her mind and body to experience what she had been denying herself for too long. It had been two years since her last sexual encounter. Her last intimate relationship had been with a guy she had met at a policeman's ball. They had dated for about a month before Symone felt comfortable enough to take their relationship to the next level. Needless to say, he got what he wanted, because she never heard from him again after that night. She didn't even bother to call him to ask why he dumped her. Symone had felt it would be a waste of time, chasing the brother down. She had felt he wasn't worth it. Since then, she had made a vow to herself. The next man who stole her heart would be her husband. Perhaps Josiah was that man.

Symone squirmed beneath Josiah's touch. Small waves erupted and overflowed onto the floor. Her mouth watered for his sweet lips; she reached up with dripping hands, grabbing his face and placing his lips onto hers. Their lips locked in a frenzied, reckless kiss. He wanted her and Symone definitely wanted him, and there was nothing or no one who could get in their way.

Josiah lifted her wet, slippery body into his arms. He carried her to the bedroom and laid her naked body across the bed.

Frantically, Symone ripped open his shirt, licking and kissing his lips, face, and neck like a love-starved woman. Every erotic thought, every unimaginable impossibility ran wild and free, as they both allowed lust and passion to overtake them.

Hastily, Josiah kicked off his shoes and stripped off his pants and underwear. He kissed her tenderly, slowly. His eyes were warm and loving as he gently entered her.

With each stroke, Symone unleashed a cry of satisfaction. The sensuous movement of her fingers on his body seemed to increase his pleasure. In response, her joy spread like the wings of a majestic eagle.

With each pulsating thrust of his manhood, Symone experienced erotic shock waves that penetrated deep down in her soul. Breathlessly she whispered, "I never thought it could be like this."

He leaned in and kissed her nose. "Believe me, if I had my way, I'd make you feel like this every day."

Symone smiled happily at the thought. "If only it were that simple. For you to make such a grand statement, I suspect we would have to be more than just bed partners, wouldn't you say?"

"Who says we're not?"

Josiah's charm, gentleness, and warmth were enough to unravel her senses completely. For the first time in her life, Symone knew what she wanted and who she wanted—and who she wanted was Josiah.

He kissed her deeply as they continued to make love.

€ ❀ ϑ

In the wee hours of the morning, Symone lay entwined in Josiah's arms. Her body had not been so relaxed in a long time. It was the annoying twinge of pain in her knee that had awakened her. Gingerly, she wiggled out from beneath his arm, reached up and turned on the small light attached to the headboard. Slowly she swung her legs over the side of the bed and got up. Her elongated shadow crept along the bedroom walls as she limped naked to the bathroom. Returning to the bed, she quietly lay back down beside Josiah. In his sleep, he rolled over onto her side of the bed. Symone admired his peacefulness as he slept. She leaned in to give him a tender kiss on the cheek; then she noticed a peculiar dark mass along his jawbone.

To get a better look, she carefully removed the small light from the headboard and shined it on Josiah's face. What she found was a bruise just under his chin. The bruise was dark and the size of a half-dollar.

She lay there for a minute contemplating. Where had he gotten it? But most importantly, how had he gotten it? She was struck by a dreadful thought.

She placed the light back onto the headboard, leaned over to the nightstand, and clicked on the lamp. She turned the light on dim, hoping its illumination would not wake him. Cautiously she got out of bed again and stepped to the foot of the bed. She gently pulled back the covers from his feet. She began to examine the lower part of Josiah's legs for bruises, like the one she had found beneath his chin.

Josiah moved suddenly. Symone froze. After he had settled back in slumber, Symone continued her examination. She carefully touched his skin for possible abrasions and lumps. Then she saw it. A discoloration on his right leg. It looked to be swollen.

A sudden uneasy feeling clutched the pit of her stomach. She stood up and put on a pair of pants and a shirt, and slipped on the complimentary slippers provided by the hotel. Then she quietly eased Josiah's car keys from his jacket pocket and walked out of the suite.

As she rode the elevator down to the garage of the hotel, she replayed in her head the struggle she had had with her attacker inside the crypt. The more she thought, the worse she felt. "Where were you really, Josiah? And if you did go to your car for a flashlight, why didn't you have it when you found me?" she said aloud.

The questions came faster and faster, but there were no answers.

She stepped off the elevator and found Josiah's Mustang right away. As she went to open the trunk, she noticed a miniature flashlight dangling from his key chain. In the back of her mind, she wondered why he had lied about that, knowing he had one on him. She couldn't understand why he had not used it in the tomb, instead of running back to his car.

She put the key in the lock and opened the trunk to the Mustang. As she began her search, Symone hoped that she wouldn't find anything that would confirm her suspicions. She hoped that her crazy misgivings were only an illusion.

She tossed tools, rags and cleaning products to one side of the trunk; there was no sign of a flashlight anywhere, big or small. But she was relentless in her search, so she continued to look. She lifted the plastic covering from the floor of the trunk, which exposed the spare tire compartment. She saw a piece of clothing. It was partly concealed beneath the spare tire, but it hung out loosely. She pulled out what turned out to be a dark jumpsuit.

She felt her head spinning. She gasped and her body trembled with fear. Her mind jetted back to the crypt, when the assailant had first run out. Symone remembered her attacker wearing something dark; it could have been some sort of jumpsuit. As she held up the garment, something fell out of the pocket and onto the cement floor by her feet. When Symone bent down to pick it up, she saw to her horror that it was a long, jagged knife stained with blood.

Twelve

Before dawn broke, Symone's hotel on Bourbon Street was swarming with cops. Inside her suite, Symone sat waiting in the living room; Josiah was still in the bedroom being questioned by DeClaud and two other Federal officers. The evidence found in the trunk of Josiah's car was deemed to be incriminating, to say the least. He dressed and was escorted out of the bedroom in handcuffs.

Symone rose to her feet as her lover was treated like the killer he was. The thought of the blood on his hands and the memory of those same hands on her body made her sick. She couldn't think straight. Her thoughts, rational and irrational, collided in her head like two speeding trains.

DeClaud led the way through the living room. Josiah shuffled across the room, accompanied by two uniformed officers. He looked lost and scared.

Symone couldn't believe this was happening. Never in a million years had she thought the man she had fallen in love with could turn out to be a cold-blooded murderer.

"Symone. Why did you do this to me?"

"Josiah, you left me no choice. I'm sorry." Her voice quivered as she held back the tears. She saw the hurt and anger in his eyes as they read him his rights and took him away.

No longer could she hold back the tears and grief that had pushed its way from the very pit of her soul. When DeClaud had dismissed every officer there, and the door had closed behind them, Symone broke down in tears.

"Oh, God! Oh my God," she wept, turning away from DeClaud, who had remained behind.

He put his hand on her shoulder and awkwardly attempted to console her. "You did the right thing, Detective." His show of concern was more than what Symone had expected, considering the fact that he and Josiah had always been at odds with one another. And DeClaud had practically found them in bed together.

"I still can't believe it. Why?" she asked.

"Nobody knows the answer to that but the killer."

Symone whirled to him. "But he's not a killer! At least not the Josiah La'Mon I know."

DeClaud stared her in the face. "What makes you think he wasn't like this all his life? Do we ever really know a person as well as we think we do, Detective?"

Symone was silent. She contemplated his words carefully.

"How could I have been so wrong? I trusted him." She felt defeated and cheated by life's circumstances and by the one man who, in a single night, had changed her life forever.

DeClaud reminded her that what she had done had been necessary. Sighing deeply, DeClaud repeated, "You did the right thing, Detective."

"Then why do I feel that I just betrayed my best friend?"

DeClaud walked to the door, opened it and stood in the doorway. "Maybe that was his plan all along. To make you his next easy victim. I'd say you were the lucky one. You got him before he could get you. Think about it. Oh, by the way. Congratulations."

"For what?" she asked bitterly.

"For solving this case. Frankly, you were the last person I thought would do it."

"That makes two of us, Lieutenant."

DeClaud walked out and closed the door behind him. Symone was left alone to deal with her troubled mind.

€ ☻ ℈

Symone could hardly close her eyes to rest. Her thoughts were on Josiah sitting in jail. She needed to see him.

The sun had barely risen in the sky before Symone found herself in a cab on her way to the precinct.

Before she arrived, it didn't dawn on her until she got there that he might not want to see her. She was sure that by now he hated her for what she had done to him.

Outside the interrogation room, behind the two-way mirror, was where she found DeClaud. He had been observing the two Federal agents questioning Josiah, who sat shackled at a table.

Symone silently walked up and stood by DeClaud.

He sipped on a cup of coffee. "I kinda knew you'd want to be here this morning," he said.

"You were right." Symone didn't even give him a glance as she stood, square-shouldered, near the glass. Her eyes were fixed on what appeared to be a very exhausted Josiah. "How long have they been in there?"

DeClaud glanced down at his Timex watch. "Not long enough. He's a tough one, that La'Mon. I'd say they've been in there a good two and a half hours."

"Why don't they give him a break? He's obviously exhausted. Look at him. He can barely hold his head up." Symone's voice shook with the intensity of her feelings.

"Detective, you're forgetting one thing. He's under arrest. This is not a resort, this is a police station. Or have you forgotten where you are?"

Symone cut a hard look at him. "No, I haven't forgotten. I know where I am and I also know that you're trying to push him over the edge with your endless questions."

"Are you trying to tell me how to run my precinct, Detective?"

"No sir, I am not. I'm just asking that you let up a little."

DeClaud chuckled sarcastically. "Why don't I just roll a big ol' comfortable bed in there along with a nice continental breakfast? Would that make you happy?"

Symone shook her head and rolled her eyes at him. All she was concerned about was getting a chance to talk to Josiah before his arraignment.

Inside the interrogation room, Josiah was bombarded with question after question.

"On the night of June 6, around eight p.m., where were you?" asked one of the agents.

Slamming his shackled hand on the side of his chair, Josiah shouted, "Aw, come on, man! You know the answer to that question!"

"Look, Josiah. Don't make this harder than it already is. Just answer the question," the fellow insisted.

Josiah was clearly fed up with all the questions. "I was at a night club," he shouted in exasperation. "It was a hectic day that day, and instead of going back to the hotel, I went to have a drink."

"Can we confirm that? Is there anyone who could vouch for having seen you?"

"I don't know. I didn't exactly sign in when I got there."

"You said you had a drink?" the other agent asked.

"Yeah. One drink."

"Well, the bartender should be able to recognize you if he saw you again, right?"

"It was a packed house. I can't say if he will or won't. You have to ask him yourself," Josiah said with a cynical smirk.

"Don't worry. We will," the agent responded strongly.

The questions seemed to go on for hours. Symone was getting fed up. "Why don't you let me talk to him, Lieutenant?"

DeClaud's head turned quickly in her direction. "Are you crazy? The last person he'd want to see is you. No. I can't do it. Considering the state of mind he's in right now, I wouldn't trust him. And you shouldn't either."

"Come on, Lieutenant. I'm the one who put him there."

"You listen here. You did good. It may not seem like it, but I'm damn proud to have you on my side. Most officers wouldn't have the balls to turn in one of their own."

"Yeah, yeah. Look. I've heard all that before. Are you going to let me go in there or aren't you? You can see they're not getting anywhere with him. Let me try. Please."

DeClaud's gaze was one of uncertainty. Symone wasn't sure if he trusted her either.

"Lieutenant, I can get through to him. Besides, I'm the only one here who's gotten close to him—and I mean close in more ways than you can imagine." She saw that DeClaud was wavering.

Finally, he nodded. "I'm gonna be right outside this door, you understand me?"

"No. When I said talk to him I meant alone. That means no watchdogs, no listening to our conversation. Just him and me."

"No. That's out of the question."

"Do you honestly think he doesn't know you're out here listening to every word that's being said? Just waiting for him to slip up? Josiah's no fool, Lieutenant. He'll make you wait until hell freezes over before he even gives you the time of day. And you think you got him exactly where you want him?" Symone laughed. "Seems to me, he's got you exactly where he wants you."

With a look of humiliation on his face, DeClaud breathed in deeply and then exhaled slowly. "You got ten minutes."

"Twenty," she spat out.

He knocked on the door and whispered to one of the agents. They left the room and Symone walked in. She stared at Josiah. He sat morosely, dressed in the clothes he had worn the night before. He was stripped of his belt and shoestrings, for fear he might harm himself.

The interrogation room was small, hot, and poorly lit, containing nothing but a few chairs and a wooden table.

Symone approached Josiah at the table. Seeing him so vulnerable and stripped of his pride made her heart ache. They had treated him like a vicious animal.

"I was wondering when you would show up," he said, through clenched teeth. "Why did you come, Symone? To see me locked up like some madman? You know I didn't kill anybody. So why? Why did you do this to me?"

Symone stood silently as he threw question after question at her, questions she wasn't prepared to answer. But there was no way around them or him. Josiah sat behind the table, his hands and feet chained to the chair. The room had no windows or air vents. The atmosphere was thick and unbearable. She saw the perspiration on his face and how it had soaked through his shirt.

Symone stood at the other end of the table. She slowly walked forward. "I had to see you."

He snorted cynically. "First, you had me arrested wrongfully, dragged out of bed, handcuffed, fingerprinted and then thrown in jail. And now you stand there and say you had to see me. Well, sorry if I can't say the same thing to you." Josiah was truly angry, and Symone couldn't blame him.

"Josiah, give me a chance to explain."

He laughed out loud. "That was a good one, Symone. You got any more good jokes like that? Did you give me a chance? Hell, no! You stood by and let them arrest me, but you did your job. You accused me of being a killer."

Symone moved closer to him. She too was angry—angry that he had made her feel worse than she was already feeling. "Josiah, if you would let me explain for a minute, you'd see I only did what any good cop would do."

"Good cop? Don't make me laugh. Any good cop would have come to me first. But I see you're still all guts and glory."

Scowling, Symone leaned in toward him and put her face in his. Angrily she said, "Do you think this is easy for me? Well, it's not. I have to think like a cop and not like a woman in love." There. She had said it. Those three little words had changed everything.

It was those words, Symone could tell, that seemed to soothe Josiah's enraged heart. He dropped his head back and tried to blink away the tears. "You don't know how I've longed to hear those words from your mouth. I love you, too, Symone. We've only known each other a couple of days, but I loved you from the first moment I saw you."

Symone's own eyes swelled with tears. "If you love me like you say you do, Josiah, then tell me the truth. Why was that bloody knife and clothing in your car?"

"Baby, you have to believe me. I don't know how it got there. Somebody must have planted it there."

"Who, Josiah? Who would do such a thing?"

"I don't know. Somebody who doesn't want this case solved. Maybe they're out to get me."

Symone paced around the room. "Why would you think that?"

"Because we were on the verge of busting their ass, that's why. You know that, Symone. You know how close we were to solving this case."

"All I know is, we were chasing a killer who, like you said, was always a step ahead of us. Frankly, I couldn't see it, but you kept insisting that somehow the killer knew our next move."

Josiah looked at her, perplexed. "And that's true. You don't believe me?"

"Josiah, right now I don't know what's true and what's not. All I know is that you've placed me in a difficult position."

"You're in a difficult position? How do you think I feel? This is a big mistake and you know it."

"All I know is that you've been lying to me."

Josiah jerked around in his chair. "Lying to you? About what, Symone?"

"What about the flashlight you said you had? As I recall, when you found me in the cemetery you weren't carrying a flashlight."

"I did have it, but I must have dropped it running to your rescue. But I did have it. If you go back to the cemetery and check, I guarantee you'll find it."

"And why did you need it to begin with?" she said, her voice heavy with accusation. "What about the little light on your key ring? Or didn't you think I'd find it?"

"Oh, for God's sake!" he burst out. "That damn thing hasn't worked for months. You found it, but did you even bother to check it?"

Symone didn't respond. She hadn't checked to see if the light worked, that's true. And if it didn't, that would explain why Josiah had gone back to his car for a flashlight.

She continued to pace the room, examining Josiah from every angle.

"How's your knee?" he asked at last.

"It's fine. And speaking of injuries, I'm curious. How did you get that bruise under your chin?"

Josiah went to touch his face, but the constraints prohibited him from reaching it. "What bruise?"

Symone stepped toward him and pointed beneath his chin. "Right there. Just below your jawbone. How did it get there?"

"I don't know. What are you trying to say?"

"I'm saying that when I was attacked back there, I distinctly remember striking my attacker in a similar place."

"How can you be sure if you hit him at all? You said yourself you didn't see him because it was dark. Are you accusing me of trying to kill you?"

Symone didn't answer him right away. "And what about that bruise on your leg? How did you get that?"

She saw that her questions were getting to him. In a sudden rage, he shook the chains that rendered him immobile. Symone was alarmed. She took a step backward.

"Do you honestly believe that I would hurt you?" he shouted.

She still didn't answer.

"Symone, look at me," he said, his voice low and demanding.

"I could never hurt you. I'd hurt myself first before I'd do anything to you."

Symone tried not to be moved by his confession. She showed no emotion. "Josiah. I'm going to ask you this and I want you to tell me the truth." She looked him straight in the eyes. "Did you kill all those people?"

"No, I didn't. Think, Symone. How do you explain what happened at that motel? If everybody thinks I'm the killer, then who was in that room?"

Symone momentarily turned away from him to contemplate his words. Could he be right? she thought. She had forgotten about the raid at the motel. Spinning on her heels, she stepped toward the door and banged on it, alerting the officer on the opposite side.

"Symone!" Josiah called out.

She turned to him. "Yes, Josiah?"

"You trusted me before. Now, with all this hanging over me, I'm asking that you trust me again. If you're as good as I know you are, then I know you'll find the real killer before he finds you. It's no mistake that this happened to me. He knows that two strands aren't easily separated." Josiah continued in a calm voice. "You're alone now, and that's what he wants. This is where you beat him at his own game. You must start thinking like him. In order to win, you must become like him."

With that in mind, Symone knocked again on the interrogation room door. It was opened to her. She didn't even glance back at Josiah. Deep down in her heart, that wasn't how she wanted to remember him.

Thirteen

"Detective. To what do I owe this pleasure?" DeClaud was in a good mood. He made his way across the room and sat behind his desk. Symone had been waiting in his office for him to return.

"Lieutenant. I need to talk to you."

"I'm all ears."

Symone sat down in front of him. She hesitated.

DeClaud looked up at her. "Well?"

"I've been thinking, sir. We've arrested the wrong man. Josiah's not a killer."

DeClaud shuffled some papers around on his desk. He seemed not to have heard what she had said. "He's gotten to you, hasn't he? That's why I didn't want you to see him."

"If you just hear me out."

"Well, I don't want to hear you out. As far as I'm concerned, we got the right man and that's all that matters."

"After re-evaluating all that's happened and the questionable circumstances, I see that it doesn't add up. Not once did you think about what happened at the motel. If Josiah's our man, then who were we chasing at the motel?"

Annoyed, DeClaud glanced at her. "What do you want me to do, let him just walk? I don't think so, Detective. You're wasting your time and mine." He continued with his paperwork.

"But—"

"Detective. I don't want to hear any more nonsense. This case if closed. Now, do you wanna find yourself on a plane back to Maryland?"

Symone stared at him in disbelief. "You wouldn't dare."

"Try me. I'm doing you a favor by letting you stay on until we can prosecute him, but if you're gonna keep suggesting that we got the wrong man, I'll send you back faster than you can say jambalaya. Just your being involved with him could jeopardize this whole case. But because you're smart, you'll keep your little affair to yourself. I want you to take some time off. You deserve it. I'll handle it from here."

Symone didn't dignify his smarmy remarks with a response. She stood up, her jaw muscles tightening in aggravation. She knew that a confrontation would only make matters worse. She opted for another approach that would be just as effective and insulting. She turned and walked out of DeClaud's office without so much as a word.

"Close my door on your way out," he snapped.

€✿Ə

Back at her hotel, Symone arranged for a rental car. When it was delivered, she drove back out to Lafayette Cemetery to search for the flashlight Josiah said he'd dropped. She retraced his steps to the point where he had found her. She searched for more than an hour and came up empty-handed. When she was about to give up, the old groundskeeper appeared from between two of the crypts and startled her. But she was relieved to see him. "I'm so glad you're here. I was wondering if you found a flashlight around here."

The old man slid back into the shadow cast by the crypt. He didn't seem to be as friendly as before. "No. I ain't seen nuthin'." He sounded nervous.

"I mean, if you could help me look for it, I would appreciate it."

Frightened, the old man declined. "I-I don't wanna talk to you no more. Go way." He turned to make his way back through the tombs.

"Please wait," Symone said. "I really need your help. My friend's life depends on finding that flashlight."

The man turned back to her, still hidden in the shadow. Slowly, he stepped out into the bright sunlight.

Symone realized why he had hidden in the shadows. The old man had been badly beaten. "Oh my God. Who did this to you?" she demanded.

He stepped away from her, retreating back into the shadows. "I'm just a clumsy ol' man."

"No. Someone's hurt you. Who was it?"

"Nobody. Leave me alone!" he cried.

"I can't do that. If this has to do with what happened here, then you're in danger."

"Please just go away. Leave me alone."

Symone moved closer, reaching out to the man. He cringed and slumped against the marble wall of the tomb, babbling hysterically. "Don't hit me no more. I won't say nuthin'. I'll be a good boy."

Symone felt sorry for him. He was clearly confused and frightened. "Ssh...Ssh. I'm not going to hurt you. Let me help you." She pulled a handkerchief from her pocket and gently dabbed a cut above his eye. "What's your name?"

"My friends call me Buc, with a 'C'.

Symone smiled at his child-like simplicity. "Okay, Buc with a 'C'. You said that I was a nice policeman. Tell me something. Did a bad cop do this to you?"

He didn't answer.

"Buc, listen to me. I'm going to show you someone. And you tell me if this is the person who hurt you." Symone pulled from her purse Josiah's shield and picture I.D. When he had been arrested in her suite, it was inadvertently left behind. She held it up to Buc. He squinted, then took hold of it and gave it a closer look. Symone held her breath as he stared at it.

He began to nod his head. "Hey. I remember him. He was the nice man that came here yesterday."

Symone was relieved. "Was this the guy who beat you?"

"Oh, no. He was nice."

Symone laughed happily. She took Buc's face in her hands and kissed him on the cheek. "Thank you. You don't know what you've just done." She had another thought. "Would you know the bad person again if you saw him?" she asked.

He nodded in agreement.

"That means he may come back. I've got to get you out of here. And he probably knows where you live, so that's not safe, either. Do you have any relatives that you could stay with?"

"None to speak of."

Symone stood up. "I have to get you out of here. If you stay that bad person might come back."

Before he could protest, Symone had taken him with her.

Later that evening at the hotel, Symone cleaned Buc up, fed him, bought him some new clothes, and put him in her bed for the night. She slept on the couch in the living room. But sleep didn't come easily. She lay awake staring at the ceiling fan slowly rotating. Her mind was on Josiah.

Fourteen

The next afternoon, Symone and Buc were headed for the New Orleans airport. Before leaving the hotel, Symone had made a phone call to Lieutenant Spaulding. She had informed him of what had happened and that she was sending Buc to him for protection. She wasn't sure she could trust DeClaud to ensure the old man's safety.

At the ticket counter she purchased a one-way ticket to Baltimore and put Buc on the plane, instructing a stewardess to keep an eye on him and make sure he got to Baltimore; someone would be waiting at the airport for him.

Symone accompanied him onto the plane. "Buc. You'll be just fine. This nice lady will take care of you."

She realized that he had not been on a plane before. His overwhelming excitement caught the attention of the other passengers.

Symone was just turning to leave the plane when he called out to her. "You're not coming with me?"

"No. I can't. I have to stay here and help my friend. But you'll be fine, I promise. And when you get there, I want you to give this to Lieutenant Spaulding. He will be waiting for you."

Symone stuffed an envelope into Buc's shirt pocket and left.

At the airport window, she watched as the plane safely left the ground. She glanced down at her watch. "One down. And one to go."

❦

It was around nine p.m. and Symone was still waiting outside the precinct in her rented car. She had been waiting hours for Lieutenant DeClaud to leave. In the darkness, she sipped apple juice through a straw and ate a seven-grain sandwich.

The police parking lot was becoming more and more like a vacant lot; one by one, officers left for home as the night progressed. There were only a few patrol cars remaining. Symone's focus was on a dark blue sedan belonging to DeClaud.

"Come on. Come on. Leave already," she mumbled. She glanced down at her watch; it was now ten o'clock. Suddenly, Symone got the break she'd been waiting for. DeClaud walked out the door and across the parking lot carrying his briefcase.

"Finally," Symone whispered.

She crouched down in the front seat of the car as he drove by. When the taillights of his car were no longer visible, Symone made her move.

She got out of her car and ran into the police station. Barnes, one of the few cops Symone had found to be easygoing and nice to her, was on the night shift.

"Detective, what are you doing here this late?" he asked.

"I left something in my desk that I need." She hated lying to him, but these were desperate times. She had to see Josiah one more time.

Barnes watched as she sat down at a desk. She had not been officially assigned to a desk, but she hoped he didn't know that. Praying that her ploy would work, she sat pretending to looking through the desk drawers.

Barnes got up from his desk, walked over and stood in front of Symone. "Hey. I heard about Josiah. Bummer. Who would have guessed?"

Symone closed the desk drawer and stood up. "Yeah, bummer."

"I also hear that you're going back to Baltimore."

"No, I'm not. The lieutenant threatened me, that's all. The lieutenant and I don't exactly see things eye to eye," she said.

"You just got to get to know him, is all. He's not a bad guy."

Symone gave Barnes a one-sided grin. "I guess I'll never know then, will I?"

"Do you need help with anything?"

"Ah, no. Thanks."

"Okay. Well, I'm gonna run to the bathroom. Yell, if you need anything."

Symone nodded politely. She couldn't wait for him to leave. When he was finally gone, Symone made her way to the holding cell where Josiah was.

As she approached the guarded door, Symone was stopped by the officer on duty. "Detective. You're not suppose to be here," he said.

"I know, but I'm leaving to go back to Maryland and I wanted to see Agent La'Mon one last time."

"You know it's against the rules to be back here after hours."

"I know, but could you let me see him this one last time?" She batted her long black eyelashes at him.

He nervously looked over his shoulder to see if anyone was looking, then let her through. "Go ahead. But make it quick."

Symone smiled and moved down the corridor to Josiah's cell. "Thanks. I owe you one," she said over her shoulder

"Yeah, yeah."

Symone watched Josiah silently from outside his cell. The eight-by-ten room hardly seemed big enough to contain all six foot, three inches of Josiah. He lay wide awake on the small, twin-size cot.

Josiah had been in jail for only a day, but he looked as if he had been in there for much longer. His faced had grown a five o'clock shadow.

He suddenly sniffed the air, looked up, and saw Symone standing there. He jumped up and rushed to her, peering at her through the cell bars, his fists curled around the cold steel. "Symone. What are you doing here?"

She could hear the relief in his voice. The smile on his face warmed her. "I've got some good news and some bad news," she said.

"Makes no difference to me." He dropped his head down in despair. "As long as I'm in here, it's all bad news."

"I wouldn't give up just yet." She moved closer to him, covering his hands with her own.

"What do I have to lose? Let's hear it."

"I went back to the cemetery and talked to Buc."

"Who's Buc?"

"You know, the old man."

"Did he find the flashlight?"

"No. But I found out something much better."

Their chattering caused the guard to look up and stare at them. Symone continued the conversation in a lower voice. "When I went back to see him he was badly beaten. But get this...he told me a cop did it."

Josiah was shocked. "Did he say who?"

"No. But the good news is, I showed him your photo I.D. and he assured me it wasn't you."

Josiah chuckled. "Hell, I could have told you that."

"But wait. Let me finish. He also said that he could identify the person who had beaten him."

"Yeah? But how do we know he won't end up floating in a river somewhere like the rest?"

"Because I sent him away."

"You did what?"

"I sent him away where he can't be found, at least not by the killer. Maybe now DeClaud will have to consider the possibility that there was somebody else at the cemetery that day besides us."

"But where does that leave me? I'm cooped up in this cement box until my arraignment. DeClaud's probably somewhere still gloating over my arrest. Nothing would make him happier than to have me put away for life."

"But you won't be locked up behind these bars for long."

"Regardless, Symone. You shouldn't have gone back there alone."

"Look. I'm trying to save you and Buc."

"Who's going to believe the word of that senile old man?"

"I believe him. And you should, too."

"I didn't say I didn't. It's just—"

"You should be happy that somebody here believes you're innocent."

"So you do believe me?"

"Yes, I do."

Josiah grinned. He and Symone took a moment to exchange an intimate glance and a gentle kiss through the bars.

"So where did you send him?" he said at last.

"To Maryland." She looked down at her watch. "Right about now, he's in good hands."

"What about DeClaud? Have you told him about all of this?"

"No. And I'm not going to, either. When I tried to tell him that you were innocent, he wanted to put me on a plane and send me back to Maryland."

"If he finds out about this, we'll both be prosecuted. Me for murder and you for conspiracy and harboring a witness."

"You're forgetting one important element here, Josiah."

"And what is that?"

"I'm trying to save your life. And right now, nothing is more important than that."

Their conversation was interrupted by the voice of the guard. "Okay, Detective. I'm afraid your time is up."

Symone responded to his command with a nod. She turned back to Josiah. "I gotta go. But I'll be back as soon as I can."

They held hands between the cell bars.

"Symone, be careful. When I get out of here, I want to be able to see you standing there waiting for me."

They shared an intimate kiss. Symone pulled his body as close to hers as possible with the obtruding bars between them. "I will. I love you, Josiah."

"Don't worry about me," he said. "I'll be fine."

Symone wiped away a tear from her cheek. "When this is all over I plan on making a career change."

He smiled. "Oh, yeah? What can be more important than being a cop?"

"Being a wife and mother," she said, looking into his eyes.

"Seems to me, you'll need a man for both of those positions. You got anybody particular in mind?" Josiah said, stroking her face.

"As a matter of fact, I do. Only question is, is he ready to make a commitment?" She searched his eyes for an answer.

"Well, if I were that man, I wouldn't let you get away," he said.

Grinning happily, she said, "Is that a fact?"

Josiah placed hands on her face. He looked deep into her eyes. "No...that's a promise."

"Well, in that case, I better get you out of here fast."

By the time Symone left the precinct, it was well after midnight. She was exhausted, but in good spirits because she had seen her lover. She kept the vision in her head of him walking out of that place a free man. She got into her car and headed back to the hotel.

Fifteen

Yawning, Symone made her way through the revolving door of the hotel. She was passing the lobby desk when she was stopped by the clerk.

"Oh, Ms. Rawlins, you have a few messages." He held up several pink pieces of paper.

Symone staggered sleepily toward him and took the messages from his hand. "Thank you. Goodnight."

"Goodnight, ma'am."

When she finally got onto the elevator, Symone tiredly collapsed against the inner wall. Her head slowly glided along the wall and rested in the corner. She closed her eyes and took a deep breath, then opened them and began sifting through the messages. But she perked up when she came across a message from Josiah. He must have convinced the guard to make the call for him, she thought.

The note read: Now faith is the substance of things hoped for, and the evidence of things not seen. I have faith in you. I love you.

Josiah was quoting Scripture out of context, but it didn't matter. The note caused a tingling, warm feeling in her heart. "I love you too, Josiah," she whispered.

The doors to the elevator opened at her floor. By this time Symone was reading the second message. It was from Omar. He wanted her to call him as soon as she got in.

"Not tonight, Omar," Symone said aloud. "All I want to do is bury my head underneath the sheets. I'll call you first thing in the morning." She pulled the key card from her purse and opened the door to her suite.

She walked in, hit the switch for the light, kicked off her shoes and tossed her bag in the chair. She was now on her third message.

Frowning at the note, she went over to the phone, picked up the receiver and began dialing. The phone on the other end of the line rang once, then twice; then on the third ring, a female's voice answered. "Josephine Street Motel, where our door is always open for you." Her chipper voice pierced Symone's ear like nails on a chalkboard.

"Yes, could I please speak to Mr. Holtz? This is Detective Rawlins returning his call."

Instead of putting Symone on hold, the young woman called out to Holtz over the phone, screaming in Symone's ear. At this point, Symone's fatigue was rapidly dissipating.

"This is Holtz."

"Mr. Holtz, this is Detective Rawlins. I received your message."

"I have the surveillance tapes you wanted to see."

Symone's stomach flipped. This was just what she had hoped to hear. "I'll be there in twenty minutes."

"I'll be waiting for you."

Symone hung up the phone, jumped into her shoes, grabbed her purse and ran out the door.

As she closed the door, she heard her phone ring. "The hell with it," she muttered.

❦ ☾ ❧

When she arrived at the motel, she flashed her badge at Mr. Holtz, the assistant manager. "Where's the tape?"

"First things first. Who's going to repair the damage to my doors?"

"Sir. You can call the station and they'll be more than happy to replace the doors," she said calmly. "But right now, I need that tape. So, if you don't mind..." She held out her hand.

"What about my protection?"

"Protection?" Symone said.

"Who's going to protect me from the killer? I was afraid to even come in here tonight."

Symone tried not to laugh in his face. She knew that in most instances, the killer never returns to the scene of the crime.

"He might come back and kill us all."

"Believe me, sir, you have nothing to worry about. You and your staff are safe."

"What about a lawsuit? What if he wants to sue me for invasion of privacy? Did you have a search warrant?"

"Sir, you have nothing to worry about." Symone didn't have time for his insecurities. She wanted the tape and she wanted it now. "Your safest place is exactly where you're standing right now. Can I have the tape, please?"

Mr. Holtz reached behind the counter and pulled out a rather large cardboard box and placed it on the counter. "I was told you wanted all the footage from the last two weeks. This is it."

Symone stared at the box. What had she been thinking? Of course it wouldn't be just a single tape. She reached out and picked up the box.

"Now that you guys got what you want, how 'bout doing something for me?"

Symone gave him a stern glance. "If you don't want to be busted, I suggest you stop while you're ahead." She hefted the box, turned and walked out of the motel.

Holtz yelled to her, "At least you can say 'Thank you'!"

Sixteen

When Symone got back to the hotel, she shot past the front desk like a bullet, carrying the heavy box of tapes to the elevator.

"Detective Rawlins!" the clerk called out to her, but Symone went straight to the elevator and punched the button.

As the door was closing, the clerk called out again. "Ma'am, I have something to tell you!" It was too late; the elevator doors shut before the clerk could relay the message.

When Symone entered the suite again, she hit the light in the foyer. She moved into the living room, tossing her jacket, keys and purse onto the sofa, then set the box of tapes on the floor in front of the TV. She was startled when the living room lights came on. She spun around, grabbed her gun and aimed it point-blank...at Omar.

"I thought I taught you better," he said, standing near the closet door.

"Man! I could have shot you." She was frightened and happy at the same time. She put her gun back in the holster and moved toward him to give him a hug. "What are you doing here?"

"I've been calling you practically all day. Where have you been?"

"You have no idea what I've been through." She marched back over to the TV and pulled a tape from the box on the floor. She checked to make sure the date written on the label was the day they raided the hotel, then slipped the tape in the VCR.

"Well, I've got some news that might make your night."

"I don't think so." Symone turned the TV on.

"You won't believe this, but—" Omar said.

"Believe me, Omar, right about now, I'll believe anything."

Omar held a large manila folder in his hand. He slid out a piece of paper and a photo. "We ran a background check into Blade's family life, just like you asked. We checked every possible court file, every rap sheet. Then it dawned on me to check his birth certificate."

Symone halted her attempt to activate the VCR. She glanced over her shoulder. "Why his birth certificate?"

"I know it sounds weird. That's what I thought at first, until..." He handed Symone a police mugshot. "I'd like introduce you to Kelly Stokes—Blade's twin sister."

Symone was floored by the news. She stepped over to the sofa and sat down in disbelief. "My God. She does look like him."

"Yeah. It's eerie, isn't it?" he said.

"I mean, if you get rid of her long hair and change her feminine features to look more manly, the resemblance is remarkable." Symone rose from the sofa. She slowly paced the floor, studying the photo.

"She's been arrested for everything," Omar said. "Petty theft, aggravated assault, breaking and entering, car-jacking—and that's when she was a teenager."

"So now she's all grown up and committing murder? But what I can't understand is, how did she get here?"

"Well, we checked for relatives, and people who knew them all said that they were ramblers. Never in one place for long. Their father left the family before she was even born and, well, we know how Blade turned out."

"What about their mother? Did you find anything on her?"

"Now this is where it gets good. The people we talked to at Kelly and her mother's last known whereabouts said that the two of them had moved in with a relative...down South."

Symone abruptly looked at Omar. "How far south?"

Omar gave her a coy grin. "You're standing in it."

"Here? In New Orleans?" she said, with wide eyes.

"That's right. The Big Easy."

Symone couldn't believe it. She had thought her fears about Blade were over. Now she had a new terror and her name was Kelly Stokes. She shivered, then slapped her forehead as a thought struck her. "Oh my God! Of course!"

Omar frowned. "What is it?"

"The carvings on the bodies."

"You mean the killer's initials?"

"They're not initials. And they're not Roman numerals, either. Kelly carved a Zodiac symbol, don't you see? The sign for Gemini. Twins!"

Omar whistled. "I'll be damned. That pretty much clinches it." He looked down into the open box of videotapes. "But what's on the tapes?"

"We're about to find out. Hit the lights, will you?"

Omar strode across the room and turned off the lights.

Symone used the remote control to activated the VCR. "When I first arrived here, Josiah informed me that the killer was a master of disguises."

"Oh, Josiah, huh? I didn't know we were on a first name basis."

Symone gave Omar a sarcastic grin. "Anyway. Two days ago, we had the killer cornered at a sleazy motel. These are the surveillance tapes from a camera overlooking

the lobby. Now, if my suspicions are right, we may have
the killer on tape."

"And you think she's on this tape?" He pointed, indi-
cating the one that was in the VCR.

"I hope so. Disguised or otherwise." Symone sat on the
edge of the sofa peering at the screen intently.

Through the night they watched one tape after another,
looking for Kelly Stokes. At last, Omar stretched and licked
his lips. "I'm hungry. What do you have in here?" He got
up from the chair and went into the small kitchen. The light
of the TV in the darkened room flickered hypnotically, as
Symone scanned each frame.

"Bingo," she whispered. She paused the tape and then
called to Omar. "Hey. Come look at this."

Omar returned with a piece of chicken, a bag of chips,
and a soda. "What did you find?"

She pointed to the man on the screen.

"Who is it?" Omar asked.

"It's Lieutenant DeClaud...with a prostitute."

"Mmm. Mmm. Talk about your power of authority. I bet
he didn't even know he was on candid camera."

"I bet he didn't either." Symone pushed play, restoring
the tape to its normal speed.

"Other than that, you find anything else?"

"No. I keep looking for anything unusual."

"Symone, you have to realize hundreds of people come
in and out of the place on a daily basis, and you can't
expect to get it the first time. We're not even a quarter way
through the tapes in that box."

"So what are you saying?"

"I'm saying we could be looking at these tapes from
now till next week this time and not see her. And it may
take a second or third run through before we do."

"Well, I suggest you make yourself comfortable, then." She took a chip from his bag. "We're going to start right now, so it's going to be a long night."

"You really feel this strongly about Josiah's innocence?"

Symone looked away. In her heart she knew she had to do everything in her power to help Josiah. "It's because of me that he's in jail right now. And it's up to me to get him out. So, yeah. I do. He's innocent and I'm going to prove it."

"I hope you know what you're getting yourself into."

She glanced at him. "I'm not doing anything you wouldn't do for me."

☾ ☀ ☽

Hours passed and dawn was fast approaching. Omar had long since fallen asleep. Symone had forced herself to stay awake even though her eyelids felt like lead. Suddenly, something caught her eye on the screen. She paused the tape and slapped her forehead. "Wake up, Omar. I've got it!"

He groggily jumped up. "What is it? What's wrong?"

"I see it now." She got up and turned on the light. She snatched Kelly Stoke's mugshot off the coffee table.

"See what?" Omar adjusted his eyes to the screen.

"The resemblance."

"Of who?"

"The prostitute that DeClaud is with. Now, tell me if I'm wrong, but don't she and Kelly look alike?"

Omar stared at the frozen image on the screen. "You can barely see her face. Plus, she has on sunglasses."

But Symone was sure. She took the photo of Kelly and placed it up against the TV screen alongside the prostitute. "You see the resemblance now?"

Omar reached into the breast pocket of his jacket behind his chair and pulled out his glasses.

"I didn't know you wore glasses," Symone said.

"These are only for reading, not for looking." He put on the glasses and moved in closer to the TV screen. "Mmm. There is a slight resemblance, but that could just be a coincidence."

"Well, that's one helluva coincidence, wouldn't you say? But that's not all. Take a look at this." She hit the eject button and took the tape from the VCR, then put in the tape from the day of the raid. She pushed the play button then paused the tape at the spot she had left it when viewing it earlier. Something about the man in the image had bothered her. "Now tell me if this is a coincidence, too."

Symone placed Kelly's photo against a man with a bushy mustache. "This person was videotaped leaving the motel just after we stormed the place."

Omar whistled. "Well I'll be damned. She looks like him, minus the mustache and wig. Probably phony."

"That's Kelly Stokes disguised as a man. She's the one who was in room 503."

"Okay." Omar grabbed the remote from her hand and turned off the TV. "Enough is enough. You've got to get some rest."

"Rest? Are you crazy? Do you realize we know who the killer is and she's been right under our noses? That's why we couldn't understand why she was always two steps ahead of us. My God, the lieutenant has been sleeping with the enemy and he didn't even know it."

Omar embraced her; he placed his hands on her shoulders and held her at arm's length. "But there's nothing you can do about it now. In the morning you can take this information to the lieutenant."

Symone allowed Omar to lead her to bed. "Josiah will be glad to hear this."

"Yes. But if you don't get some sleep, you won't be around to catch anybody. You're dead on your feet from exhaustion. Good night. I'll sack out on the sofa." He turned to leave the bedroom.

"Omar," she began.

He turned to her. "Yeah?"

"I'm glad you're here."

He smiled. "So am I. Somebody has to look after you."

Seventeen

The next morning, Symone was up, dressed and almost out the door before Omar caught her.

"Where do you think you're going?" he asked.

"I gotta talk to the lieutenant. I called the station, but he wasn't there. So I'm going to his house."

Omar got up from the sofa. "You don't quit, do you?"

"No, I don't. Now are you coming with me or not?"

"I'm going with you."

As they were about to get into the elevator, they were met by one of the housekeepers in the hallway.

"Good morning," the young woman said.

Symone stopped her. "Excuse me."

"Yes, ma'am?"

"I haven't seen Tina, the other housekeeper, in about a four days. Is she ill?"

"Tina, ma'am? I'm sorry, I don't know who that is."

"She's the housekeeper I met when I arrived here. You know—red hair, glasses. She was really nice."

The young woman looked bewildered. "I don't know any 'Tina'. Maybe you can ask down at the front desk."

The housekeeper walked away, pushing her laundry cart. Symone stood in the middle of the hall, just as bewildered.

When Symone and Omar reached the lobby, they could smell the aroma of freshly brewed coffee. There was an early-morning buzz of conversation going on in the corner, where a continental breakfast table had been set up.

"I'm going to get a cup a coffee. You want anything?" Omar asked.

"No. You go ahead."

While Omar went to get some coffee, Symone made her way to the front desk. "Excuse me. Do you have an employee working in housekeeping by the name of Tina Fisk?"

The day-shift clerk went into the back and brought out the supervisor. "What seems to be the problem, ma'am?"

"I would like to know if you have an employee working housekeeping who goes by the name of Tina Fisk."

"Ma'am, I've been working at this hotel for fifteen years. I know everyone who works here or who's come and gone, but I've never heard of a Tina Fisk."

Symone felt as if the floor had dropped from under her.

Omar approached her. "So what's up?"

Turning her back on the two men behind the desk, Symone whispered to Omar, "They never heard of a Tina."

"Are you sure you have the right name?"

Symone responded through tight lips, "Yes, I have the right name."

"Think, Symone. If Kelly Stokes had a disguise on the tape, what makes you think she didn't wear one with you?"

Symone looked away in disgust. What a gullible fool she'd been. You're right, Omar. She could very well have been wearing one. I guess I was hoping that Tina was nothing more than a harmless young girl."

"Now you know" He gently caressed her shoulder. "Come on. Let's go."

Symone and Omar left the hotel and headed for DeClaud's house.

For about ten minutes, they rode in silence. Then Omar broke the ice. "You sure are quiet over there."

Turning with a wry grin, Symone responded, "Would you believe I'm praying?"

"What's so hard to believe?"

"I haven't prayed in over a year. I had convinced myself that after Jordan died there was no one to pray to."

"There's always someone to pray to, Symone. You just have to open your mouth and speak."

"It's not as easy as it sounds."

"I have to admit that. I never gave prayer much thought until I realized that I could have lost my kid."

"I've been so preoccupied with this case, I never once asked you about Monica and the baby."

"They're both fine. In fact, the doctors are sure that she'll go full term."

"That's great."

"Yeah, we were lucky."

"I hope to be so lucky some day, to have what you and Monica have."

"You will. And that man will be the luckiest guy in the world." Omar reached over and gently squeezed her hand.

At last they pulled up in front of Lieutenant DeClaud's suburban home. His car was still parked in the driveway.

Symone and Omar got out and approached the house casually. The neighborhood was like any other neighborhood. Large family homes with one or two car garages, a playground and kids on a typical, quiet summer's day.

Symone and Omar rang the doorbell. They waited for DeClaud to answer.

"Doesn't seem like he's home," Omar commented as he tried to look in one of the windows. "Maybe he took the bus."

"The lieutenant is not the public transportation type."

Investigating other windows around the house, Omar disappeared for a moment, then returned. "The back door is open."

They cautiously moved to the back of the house with guns drawn. As they took their positions, Omar pushed the door with his hand. The door drifted open slowly and they went in.

Symone called out. "Lieutenant? It's Detective Rawlins and Detective Harris." The two split up. Symone went to find the bedroom and Omar went into the living room.

When Omar entered the living room, it was in shambles. Furniture had been turned over, papers and books were everywhere. "I guess we can rule out him calling in sick," he said, loud enough for Symone to hear.

Symone found the bedroom a wreck as well. She stepped over debris and broken glass. The pillows on the bed were slashed, the bedding was thrown on the floor, the contents of the closet had been scattered everywhere, and the dresser drawers were tipped open.

Symone couldn't believe what she was seeing. She wondered if the lieutenant himself had been the victim of foul play. Or had he simply made it look that way?

As she trod amid the clutter, Symone accidentally tripped over an object hidden beneath a blanket on the floor. She bent down and, using the barrel of her gun, lifted up the bedding. There, buried under the covers was a long, black flashlight. Pulling a handkerchief from her pocket, Symone picked up the flashlight, careful not to leave fingerprints.

Examining the flashlight, she turned it over and found the initials "J.L." embossed on the side of the barrel.

"J.L. Josiah La'Mon," she whispered. "So you were telling the truth."

She returned to the living room and Omar. "You find anything?" Symone walked up beside him. He held a small photo in his hand.

"It's a picture I found in the back of his desk drawer."

Symone took the picture from his hand. It was a photo of DeClaud and a woman. "I'll be damned. She looks exactly like the girl I found in my room the first day I checked into the hotel. Put a pair of glasses on her and pull her hair up, she would be a dead ringer," she said, examining the photo more closely. "I'm even going to go out on a limb and say that Tina Fisk is definitely Kelly Stokes."

Omar pulled out the photo of Kelly and held it against the one in Symone's hand. "You could be right."

"So, she knew who I was all along. That's how she stayed two steps ahead of the game."

"Yeah, I would think screwing a lieutenant of the police department would have its advantages," he said. He glanced at the flashlight in Symone's hand. "What's that?"

"Josiah's flashlight. He told me he dropped it at he cemetery."

"Where did you find it?"

"In the lieutenant's bedroom. I'm taking it with us. It will help to clear Josiah."

"We had better get to the station fast," he said with a concerned look.

"My sentiments exactly. Let's go."

Eighteen

Symone and Omar jumped out of the car and burst through the department doors like the Mod Squad. The station was in a state of pandemonium. The officers had gathered together in the squad room. They were all shouting and out-talking one another.

"What the hell is going on here?" Symone yelled above the commotion. Officer Barnes walked over to where Symone and Omar stood. "What's going on, Barnes?" she repeated.

"We just got an anonymous tip that the lieutenant has been kidnapped."

"What?"

"But that ain't all," he said and looked at Omar questioningly.

Symone saw the apprehension on his face. "It's okay. This is Detective Harris, my partner from Maryland."

Barnes nodded, then he reached out and shook Omar's hand. "Nice to meet you, sir. Like I was saying. Not only is the lieutenant missing but..." he hesitated.

"What?" Symone said impatiently.

"It's Agent La'Mon."

Her eyes widened from fear. "What about him?"

"He's gone."

"Gone? What do you mean gone?" She grabbed Barnes by the arm. "Gone where?"

"That's it. We don't know."

Symone pushed past him and stormed toward the holding cell area. She found Josiah's cell empty, just as Barnes had said.

"Where is he?" Symone shouted.

Barnes walked up beside her. "All we know is that we found the guard unconscious inside Agent La'Mon's cell. From what he told us after regaining consciousness, we figure he was hit over the head, dragged and locked in the holding cell."

"Where is the guard now?"

"An officer took him to the hospital. He was bleeding pretty bad on his head. We asked him if he knew who did it. He said he didn't see his attacker."

Symone was at a loss. She didn't know what to do at this point. She only hoped for a miracle.

"But," Barnes interjected, "there was something we found that you might want to see." He went behind the guard's desk, opened a drawer and pulled out an object. He handed it to Symone. "We didn't know what to make of it at first, but I think the note says it all."

Symone was staring at a tiny replica of an electric chair with a note attached to it. The note read: "Tick Tock. You're in for quite a shock!" The words on the paper angered her. "That bitch," she said through clenched teeth. "I know what she's planning to do."

"She, Detective?" Barnes asked, surprised.

"Yeah. It's not a man like we all thought. It's a woman. Her name is Kelly Stokes. She's the twin sister to a serial killer we executed over a year ago."

"So, what does this mean?" he asked.

"She's planning to execute them just like we executed her brother."

"But how could one woman handle two men? It's impossible...isn't it?"

"With the proper training and strength to match, one person can take out five people, regardless of their size." Symone looked down at the trinket again. She held onto it as if to get some sort of vibe from it. "I know why she's doing this."

"Please, enlighten us all," Barnes said.

"This isn't about Josiah or the lieutenant. This is about me and her wanting retribution for what I did to her brother. Don't you see, Omar? She wants revenge. And what better way to get to me than through Josiah?"

"Well, what about the lieutenant? Are you implying that he is somehow connected?" Barnes said in disbelief. "The lieutenant is one of the good guys." Barnes obviously had more faith in DeClaud than she had.

"Don't go defending him just yet. We're still not sure of his involvement here. Maybe he's just a pawn she needed in her little game, or he has been connected all along. So we're not ruling out anything. But we won't find anything out standing here, will we?"

"So what do we do now?" Omar asked.

The wheels were in motion in Symone's head. She recalled Josiah's advice. To defeat the enemy, you must think like him and you must become him. She turned to the two men. "We give her what she wants."

"And that is?" Barnes asked skeptically.

Symone glanced at Omar. "Me."

"Whoa! Wait a minute, Symone," Omar interrupted. "It's obvious that this woman wants to kill you."

"Precisely. But how else do we get Josiah and the lieutenant from her clutches? I know she wants to kill me, and I'm not happy being a sitting duck. But what choice do I have at this point?"

"So what's the game plan?" Barnes asked anxiously.

Symone shrugged her shoulders. "I don't know. First of all, we don't know where they are. Secondly, we don't know if they're still alive."

"Well, do you have any idea where she might be? I mean, if she wants you to come after her, where would she go? A place where she would have full advantage over you. There has to be something you can go on," Omar said.

Symone suddenly got an idea. "Barnes, I want you to assemble every available officer and meet me in the squad room in ten minutes. But before you do that—" Symone turned to Omar. "Do you have that picture of Kelly on you?"

"Right here." He pulled the photo from his jacket and gave it to Symone.

"Barnes, I need you to make some copies of this picture and give it to every officer out there."

Barnes took the photo, turned on his heel and jetted back out front.

Symone paced in a circle inside the empty cell.

Omar glanced at her questioningly. "What are you thinking, Symone?"

"I'm thinking there could only be one place she could be holed up at. It's a long shot, but what do we have to lose?"

"Do you mind telling me where this place is?"

"Lafayette Cemetery."

Barnes had got together a dozen or so officers. He had even called in a S.W.A.T. team. Everyone was waiting for Symone when she and Omar finally joined them.

She briefed the men in blue. "It's no secret that we have a very dangerous situation here. I first want to say that I am not trying to take the place of the lieutenant. But I am going to do whatever humanly possible to get our own back alive. Each of you has a copy of the picture of our killer. And don't be fooled by her appearance. This woman is a killer without a conscience. She has two of our own in her grasp and we're going to get them back." Symone looked into the faces of her fellow officers and saw loyalty and trust. She knew that they would follow her anywhere. She was grateful to them and to Omar, who stood by her side.

"Look, guys," she went on. "I don't know how it's going to turn out here. I would just like to say that during my time here, you all made me feel a part of the team. And I would go to hell and back if anyone of you were in trouble. So I'm asking you, don't be a hero on my account. I want this to be a zero-casualty mission. I know I don't have to say how this case has become personal to me, but I have someone I care for, and I want him back safe and alive. So no heroics, okay? And watch each other's back out there."

When she had finished her speech, Symone got a surprising round of applause. She grinned and waved the men away. Everyone ran to his patrol vehicle.

Omar just stood there and looked at her. "If I didn't know any better, I'd swear you were after the lieutenant's job."

Symone checked her gun and placed it back in her holster. "Please. That's the last thing I want to be. Besides, after this, my cop and robber days are over. And you can quote me on that."

They joined a fleet of roaring vehicles outside the station. Symone and Omar rode together. She put her hand out the window of the car and signaled the convoy. The twirling red, blue and white lights flashed like a string of Christmas lights through the streets. The blaring sirens rang out in a deafening pitch.

Nineteen

A few curious tourists gathered as the fleet of police cruisers skidded to a screeching halt along the block containing
Lafayette Cemetery. Symone and Omar flagged down the
S.W.A.T. vehicle, directing it to the iron-gated entrance to
the cemetery. The special task forces team jumped out,
dressed for battle. Symone split the officers into four teams,
equipping each with a radio.

"It's like a maze in there, so be careful. Each of you has
a walkie-talkie. I expect you to use it to stay in touch with
me and with your team. Use caution. Like I said before, I
don't want any heroes, just survivors. Got it?" She dis-
persed the groups, and they filed through the gate.

With guns drawn, Symone and Omar led a team of
eager and well-trained officers into what she hoped would
be the beginning of the end.

Symone had a hunch that they wouldn't have to search
every square inch of the cemetery to find Kelly Stokes. She
had already given them the clue where they would find
her.

"Omar," she began, keeping her voice low as they
worked their way among the tombs, "she wants me to find
her. In fact, she's not hiding at all. She's making it easy for
me to find her. She knew there would be one place I was
certain to check."

"And that's where, exactly?" Omar hurried in her footsteps.

"The tomb where she attacked me."

Slowly, Symone led Omar and the team of officers to the solitary crypt where she and Kelly Stokes had met before.

Symone whispered to Omar. "If anything should happen to me, I want you to—"

"Ssh. Nothing is going to happen to you. I promise."

"But just in case."

"Will you shut up? Your mouth is going to get both of us killed."

"I just want you to know that I love you," she said. "You're like family to me. I just wanted you to know that."

Omar rolled his eyes upward in annoyance. "All I know is, after we catch this wench, we're on the first plane back to B-more."

Symone motioned to the other officers to stay back as she cautiously peered around the tomb to her right. They had reached the open plot in the cemetery that held the large crypt where she had been attacked. Symone silently pointed to it. Omar signaled for the other officers to remain hidden in the shadows of the smaller tombs surrounding the plot, and he and Symone began to approach the crypt.

Suddenly, Omar stopped. He raised his finger to his ear. Symone stood dead in her tracks to listen. From several feet away, they heard the low rumble of a motor. It sounded almost like a lawnmower.

Symone checked the safety on her 9mm and glanced at Omar. They darted up to the door and stood with their backs against the cold marble wall. They tried not to make a sound.

Symone held her weapon close to her chest, ready to fire at any moment. The sound of the motor was coming from inside the tomb. She looked at Omar, and nodded toward the other officers awaiting instructions back in the shadows of the smaller tombs. Omar silently motioned for them to take up positions around the plot. Quickly, the rest of the team fell into place and took their positions. Handguns and M16's were pointed at the entrance to the tomb from all directions.

Symone was ready to get it over with. She mouthed the count of three, then called out "Kelly!" in a loud voice.

There was a brief moment of silence. Omar looked at her and winked as he always did before taking down their man.

Symone took a deep breath and called out to the enemy again. "Kelly Stokes, this is NOPD. We have you surrounded. Surrender or we'll be forced to come in and get you."

They waited for a response or a sign. When there was none, Symone readied herself to go in. She nodded to Omar, who slowly reached out and pushed on the iron door of the tomb. With a squeak, it swung open.

With their guns ready to fire, Symone and Omar quickly darted into the tomb, taking up positions on either side of the door with their backs against the wall. Symone couldn't believe what she was seeing. There was a utility light hanging from an extension cord draped over a marble vase protruding from the far wall. The motor they had heard was from a small portable generator running quietly in the corner. Josiah and DeClaud were sitting side by side on two metal chairs. Their mouths were taped and their hands were bound behind their backs. Their ankles were tied and their bare feet had been placed in two metal buckets filled with water. On their heads, the two men wore a strange headband with wires attached to it. Cables from the headbands, as well as the metal buckets, were connected to—

"Oh my God," Symone said aloud, as Kelly Stokes stepped out of the shadows. She was holding a switch of some sort, the cables running from it to the generator and to Josiah and DeClaud.

Kelly Stokes was not playing around. She intended to electrocute Josiah and DeClaud.

"Well, well, well," Kelly said, "look who decided to show up for the party after all."

After all the photos and disguises she had worn before, Symone wasn't sure if this was the undisguised Kelly or not. Symone didn't want to make any sudden moves. "I wouldn't have missed this for the world," she said suppressing the anger that rose up inside her. The last thing she wanted was a confrontation. If at all possible she wanted to take Kelly alive. "I see you went ahead and started without me," she said nonchalantly as she carefully moved closer. "I have to hand it to you, you outdid yourself with this one." She was amazed at the extreme measures her nemesis had gone to.

"That's far enough." Kelly said, in a sharp tone.

Symone stopped cold. She kept a close eye on Kelly but, at the same time, she gave Josiah an encouraging smile. From where she stood, which wasn't far from Josiah, she saw that he was not seriously hurt. Aside from a couple of bruises and a cut on his cheek, he seemed fine. But DeClaud was clearly injured. He sat in the chair, stripped of his shirt, and bleeding. Kelly had left her mark on him— the familiar carving of the Gemini, cut deep across his chest. "Okay, Kelly. Or should I say Tina?" Symone said.

"I really had you fooled, didn't I?" Kelly smirked deviously. Symone saw she was enjoying her little game. "Especially when I led you to believe that I was actually trying to help you," she said with a laugh. "You're a bigger fool than I thought."

Symone glanced at Josiah. She saw that he was inconspicuously trying to free himself. Their eyes connected.

Symone felt him giving her strength as she stalled for time. All she really wanted to do was drop Kelly where she stood, but the woman had that damned switch in her hand.

"Are you sure you aren't helping me now?" Symone tried to confuse her. "But I have to admit, you did have me fooled. I actually believed you in the hotel."

"Yeah. Who would of thunk it that the brave and clever Detective Rawlins would fall for a bunch of crap like that? I should have taken you out right then and there. You wouldn't of known what hit you."

"Then why didn't you? I mean, you had every opportunity, not to mention a great disguise. The poor helpless maid."

"No. There's a time and place for everything. And seeing that I had nothing but time on my side, I waited and waited until the time was right."

"What I can't figure is, how did you know I would be staying at that particular hotel?"

"That was easy. I knew you had to have a reservation, so I called, checking every hotel that was in a mile radius of the police station. And boom, there you were. Then, it was just a matter of time before you figured out that my brother had a twin."

It was obvious to Symone that Kelly was much more clever than her brother, Blade. This one had a well-executed plan. "I'm impressed."

Kelly took a half bow. "Thank you. That means a lot, coming from a hero like yourself."

"I'm not a hero. I did what I was trained for. But you, you don't have to do this. Haven't you killed enough innocent people already?"

Kelly snorted. "Are you kidding? This is my greatest performance ever. I had to keep going until I got the catch of the day."

"And what's that?"

"To have you on your knees, begging me for mercy. Frankly, that's more then what you gave my brother when you had him killed."

"No. Your brother got himself killed. But I see you're birds of a feather."

That seemed to anger Kelly, who viciously toyed with the switch.

Symone didn't want to show Kelly that she feared for her friends' lives, and she didn't want to provoke her. She inched toward the woman, warning Omar with a glance that he was to do nothing. "Wait a minute, Kelly." She lowered her gun in a show of good faith. "Before you go and do something you'll regret, let's talk it out."

"What makes you think I want to talk to you? I hate you."

"At least tell me why you kidnapped a federal agent and the lieutenant. You owe me at least that much."

Kelly looked at Symone with squinted eyes. She had not once taken her finger off the switch. "Because eventually you would have figured me out. And it was too soon."

"So you planted those things in the trunk of Agent La'Mon's car to throw us off?"

"Wasn't that beautiful? I even had you confused about him."

"Yeah, you did. But why the lieutenant? You were already sleeping with him. Why this? You had him fooled all this time."

"Because he was beginning to bore me."

"But the picture of you and him together. You two looked so much in love."

Symone saw the sudden jerk of DeClaud's posture. He sat sweating profusely, looking at Symone, then Omar, with embarrassed eyes.

Kelly laughed. "Love? He doesn't love me and I sure as hell don't love him." She struck DeClaud in the back of the head with her elbow. "Just look at him. Sweating like a big fat pig. All he wanted was sex. So I saw this as the perfect opportunity to get what I wanted from him. He turned out to be more useful than I imagined."

"So he wasn't helping you?"

"Helping me? Please. He could hardly help himself out of bed when I finished with him."

"Speaking of which, you were the one who called and gave us that tip about the motel, weren't you?

Kelly suddenly stomped her foot with enthusiasm. "Hallelujah! Give that girl a cigar. You figured it out."

Symone chuckled from the revelation as well.

"Tell me. How did you put it all together?" Kelly asked.

"The clues. You made it too easy. The listing of cemeteries in the telephone book, the obvious escape down the laundry chute. You were testing us," Symone said.

"You're right. I just wanted to see how well you follow directions. And you did, perfectly."

"But what about our first encounter here? Why didn't you kill me then?"

"Anxious, aren't we?" Kelly said, in a childish manner. "I didn't want to. Na-na-na-na-na. I wanted to scare you. Were you?"

Symone didn't answer right away. Her jaw tightened and she felt her body temperature rise. "Yeah. I was scared," she said at last. She saw a gratifying smile appear on the woman's face. "What about the other questions?"

"This one I'll give you for free," Kelly said. "How was I able to get both men? Well, let's see. First, I called ol' fat face here, and told him that I had some urgent news about the murders. I told him that I had met a guy who confessed to killing the people. I pretended to be afraid for my life

and I would only talk to him and Agent Columbo, here."
She chuckled wickedly. "You'd be surprised at what sex
can make a man do. The fat fool even bashed his own cop
to spring the fed boy from jail!"

Symone swallowed her disgust. "And the mess at
DeClaud's place?"

"Hell, I only did that for fun. And to confuse you." At
her words, Omar muttered a curse.

"What happened when they met you? Symone persisted.

"When they got to my apartment, I drugged 'em. See?
It was that easy. I dragged 'em to my car, and *voila*—here
we are."

"And I guess it's safe to say you beat the old man as
well?" Symone asked.

Kelly responded with a cheap grin and a nod. "Dressed
up like a cop to do it, too. I had to keep him quiet. He
was beginning to get too nosey."

Symone had finally gotten what she wanted—a full confession. "I guess we both underestimated each other,
wouldn't you say, Kelly?"

"I wouldn't say that. I didn't underestimate you.
Besides, I'm still holding the cards, wouldn't you say,
Detective?" Kelly glanced at the switch in her hand.
"Oops...I mean holding the switch."

Symone was fed up with her games. It was time to put
the bitch out of her misery. Symone managed to chuckle at
Kelly's remark. "That was a good one. But I got one for
you. What makes you think you're going to get out of here
alive when there are cops all around you? You have no
way out."

Kelly's grinning face turned sour. "I don't care if I get
out alive or not. Thanks to you, I have nothing left but
revenge. So," she looked at Josiah and DeClaud, "say

good-bye to the nice detective, gentlemen." Kelly was about to apply pressure to the switch when Symone yelled out.

"Kelly, wait! Why kill them when you got me? I mean, that is what you've been waiting for, right? The ultimate prize. Your brother failed to get me, but you can." Symone then did the unthinkable, ignoring the look of horror on Omar's face. She laid her gun on top of the granite vault that sat in the center of the room. She lifted her hands shoulder height and began to walk slowly around the vault toward Kelly.

Omar frowned at Symone, then at Kelly, then Symone again. "Symone, what are you doing?" His hand firmly gripped his weapon.

"This is between me and her, Omar. Drop your gun."

"I will not!" he responded defiantly.

"Just do it, Omar!" Symone screamed back at him.

Omar reluctantly obeyed and dropped his weapon.

Symone walked closer and closer. "See, Kelly? I'm unarmed. I'm surrendering to you." She saw the ambivalence in Kelly's eyes. She knew that the woman wanted to flip the switch.

"No need to take this any further," Symone continued. "I'm here just like you planned. Take me out. Come on. You tried to before. Here's your chance for a rematch." Symone taunted and pushed her to make a move. Their determined eyes were fastened on each other.

At that moment, a bird flew in, distracting everyone. In that split second, Kelly relaxed her fingers on the switch. With quick reflexes, Symone reached behind her back pulled out her backup .38 and fired, hitting Kelly in the chest. The switch flew in one direction and Kelly fell in the other. Omar lunged forward, catching the switch in the palm of his hands.

Twenty

The pungent smell of burnt gunpowder filled the tomb, and everyone's ears were ringing from the shot. DeClaud sat sobbing, his cries muffled by the tape across his mouth.

Symone approached Kelly, who lay on the floor of the tomb. She crouched down beside the woman. Strangely enough, Symone felt sorry for her.

Kelly tried to talk. Blood flowed from her mouth and down the side of her cheek.

"Don't try to speak. Call the paramedics!" Symone called to one of the half-dozen officers who had stormed in after the shot.

Kelly coughed up blood. "No. Let me die," she said in a cracked voice.

Symone stared down into the face of the young woman who, by every right, deserved death. For Symone, this was the final scene of a tragic story she had been living for too long. She'd come to the end of another chapter in her life. This time it was finally over for sure.

Kelly lay there dying. Omar walked up beside her. "An ambulance is on its way."

Symone did something that even seemed to surprise Omar. She reached down, took Kelly's hand and held it as she died. "It is finished," Symone whispered. "This time, it is finished."

When the paramedics finally arrived, they carted Kelly's body to the nearest hospital. In the meantime,

DeClaud and Josiah had their wounds looked at and cared for.

Symone and Omar stood by as the tomb was blocked off and enclosed by the bright yellow tapes used at crime scenes. The door of the tomb was shut for good.

"Well, here's to another job well done. You were right. Well, almost right," Omar said.

Symone turned to him with a questioning look on her face. "I was almost right about what?"

"You said no casualties."

"Ahhh. But I was right technically. 'Cause you see I didn't lose any of my men. Everyone's here and accounted for."

"Right. Right." Omar hesitated.

Symone glanced at him. "What? Why are you looking at me like that?"

"After all the tight spots and dangerous encounters we've been through together, you still manage to amaze me."

"I do, don't I?" she said with a triumphant grin. "I tell you, boy. Sometimes I amaze the hell out of myself."

"What you did back there, holding her hand as she died," he said, shaking his head in disbelief. "I don't think I could have done it."

Symone faced him squarely. "We never realize how precious life is until it's taken away. What I did in there was for her and for me. Her life ended today. But you know, I feel like mine is just beginning."

Omar pulled her into his arms and held her tight. "I am so proud of you."

Symone felt the tears swell up behind her eyes, but she held them back. "Thanks. And I appreciate you, too. If you hadn't come when you did, I don't know if things would have turned out so well."

"Oh, get out of here. You know you had this whole case under control."

Symone chuckled. "Yeah, right."

"For a minute there, I thought she was going to turn the juice on those guys."

"So did I. But as usual, my quickness prevailed," she said smugly. "Again, I've proven that I can outshoot you anytime, anywhere, even on my knees." She gave Omar a wicked grin, then walked to Josiah, who was leaning up against an ambulance.

He greeted her with open arms. "Mmm. It's so good to hold you again." He kissed her.

Symone couldn't have been happier. She had gotten her life back and her man back all in the same day. Life was good again. "For a second there, I thought she had you," she said.

"Believe me, I thought she had me, too. But I knew you would come to my rescue."

For the first time in a long time, Symone let out a hearty laugh. "Oh, you did, did you?"

Josiah pulled her closer to him. "Yep. I could feel you as you got closer and closer to this spot."

"Now, you're not gonna get all spooky on me, are you? Because if you are, I've had just about enough—" Josiah shut her up by kissing her. The kiss was passionate and sexy.

Omar approached the two lovebirds. He purposely cleared his throat to get their attention.

Symone was embarrassed, and she knew Josiah felt the same. They abruptly stopped kissing and wiped the saliva off their lips.

"Uh, excuse me." Omar said. "But I was just wondering if you guys are ready to leave this place. 'Cause frankly, I've had just about enough for one day."

The couple shared a mutual "Yes!"

DeClaud, technically under arrest for assaulting an officer and aiding a prisoner to escape, took a ride to the hospital for stitches in his chest wounds, while Symone, Josiah and Omar rode back to the hotel together.

❈❈❈

Two weeks passed before the case was officially closed. Symone and Omar had stayed in New Orleans for a little rest and relaxation. The Big Easy was finally back to normal.

The mayor and the commissioner of the city celebrated with a pinning ceremony in honor of the brave men and women who had put their lives on the line to save the city. Symone, Josiah, and Omar were the real heroes. As a surprise to Symone and Omar, their superior, Lieutenant Spaulding, had been flown in for the event. A reception for the entire city was held on the grounds of City Hall.

DeClaud was still under investigation, and his men had rallied around him, promising to testify on his behalf. Symone had had no contact with him since that day in the tomb, but she knew that Barnes and some of the others had persuaded him to come to the reception, since—except for his unfortunate involvement with Kelly Stokes—he had handled the case with distinction. And the full story had been kept from the newspapers.

Spotting DeClaud across the lawn, Symone took the liberty of introducing Spaulding to him. "Lieutenant, this is Lieutenant DeClaud." The two men shook hands.

"Nice to finally meet you, Lieutenant DeClaud," said Spaulding.

"You got yourself two of the finest officers this town has ever seen, Spaulding." DeClaud nodded toward Symone.

"Well, I'm kinda proud of them myself. Good officers are hard to come by these days," Spaulding said, placing his arm around Symone's shoulders. "I wouldn't trade them in for a million bucks."

"I can understand why," DeClaud said.

Symone wrapped her arm around Spaulding's waist. "Thanks for coming, Lieutenant."

"Are you kidding? I wouldn't miss this for the world. To have two of my best officers represent Baltimore, Maryland, is an honor in itself."

Symone hugged him. "See? That's why I love being a cop. I get to work with great people like Omar."

"Well, as I hear it, you and Lieutenant DeClaud worked hard, side by side."

Symone didn't respond; she just looked into DeClaud's face and smiled blandly. DeClaud, clearly embarrassed, diverted his eyes downward. Symone knew the truth. DeClaud had given her a hard time from the moment she had stepped foot into his office, not to mention his law breaking.

"Well, sir, you heard right," she said at last.

DeClaud immediately perked up and gave her a grateful smile.

"Lieutenant DeClaud," she went on, "if I didn't say it before, I'll say it now. It's been a pleasure working with you, sir. And if I had to do it all over again, I would." She extended her hand to him. They shook hands. Symone could tell that he was genuinely moved; he was misty-eyed.

Spaulding patted them both on the back. "DeClaud, looks like you've made a friend for life."

"I hope so," the lieutenant said fervently.

Spaulding excused himself and left the two alone.

Symone could see that DeClaud felt awkward at their being alone.

"Uh...I really want to thank you for everything," he said.

"Don't mention it, sir. I was only doing my job." Symone spoke straightforwardly.

"No. Even I have to admit that I was wrong about you, and I apologize."

"Forget about it. It's all in a day's work. Or should I say week's work. Besides, you have a great department and they're all behind you one hundred percent. I'm sure you would have done the same for me if the tables had been turned."

"Mmm. I wouldn't put that much trust in me if I were you. In my old age, you've taught me the meaning of friendship and trust. I'll never forget what you've done for me and this city, Detective." He held out his hand again. Symone accepted his hand and his friendship.

"Sorry it ended so badly for you," Symone said, a note of genuine concern in her voice.

"Well, I guess that's my punishment for not being more scrupulous in my personal life. I let my emotions overrule my common sense as a cop."

"Don't worry about it, Lieutenant. Take it from me, we all make mistakes. And if I can put in a good word for you, I will."

Symone left DeClaud with the commissioner and walked over to where Josiah and Omar stood talking. She hung back to eavesdrop on their conversation, finding a large tree to hide behind.

"I'm glad I met you before things got really messy," Omar said sarcastically.

"So do I." Josiah laughed. "I want to thank you for taking care of Symone when I was unable to."

"Well, she was determined to find you, no matter what. That's how she is. Once she gets her teeth into something, it's hard for her to let go."

"I get the feeling you're not just talking about work, are you?" Josiah said.

Omar threw his arm around Josiah's shoulders. "No, my man. I'm not talking about work. It seems to me there's more going on between you two than anyone knows."

"Is it that obvious, Omar?"

"Just let me say this: For starters, that lip-lock you two were in at the cemetery was off the scale. Now, to me, that wasn't just any ordinary kiss. Nope. That was an 'I got you and I ain't letting you go' kind of kiss."

Josiah chuckled like a big kid. "Come on, man, stop playing."

"I'm serious, man. You got her eating out of the palm of your hand."

"You really think so? I mean, I've never met a woman like her. I'm thinking about spending the rest of my life with her."

Omar stepped back in surprise. "Are we talking relationship here, or are we talking marriage?"

Josiah leaned toward Omar. "I'm talking about the ol' ball and chain bit, the his and hers towels, the joint checking account, the rings and all."

Omar slapped a spirited high-five with Josiah. "Have you asked her yet?"

"Not yet. I was hoping to ask her before the day is out."

"You may not have to wait much longer." Omar spotted Symone behind the tree and motioned her in their direction. "Here's your chance to ask her now."

"Hey, now. What's happening?" Symone said innocently, moving toward them.

"You're sure in a good mood." Omar playfully pinched her cheek.

"I feel great." Symone was on top of the world. Nothing could spoil this day, she thought. She leaned into Josiah's side and embraced him. "And what have you two been talking about? I can tell by the look on your faces that it must have been something interesting, because Omar looks like the cat who swallowed the canary."

"What? I can't be happy, either? I'm like you. I'm feeling good. How about you, Josiah, man?" Omar raised his eyebrows peculiarly. "How you feeling?" He seemed to be giving Josiah a secret signal.

Josiah took Symone's hands and got on one knee, ignoring everyone who was looking their way. "Symone. I've been wanting to ask this forever, it seems like. From the first moment I saw you, I knew you were the one. And I know that sounds cliché-ish, but I don't know how else to say it. So before you have a chance to think about it, I want to know if you would do me the honor of becoming my wife."

Symone's eyes filled with tears of joy. For a second or two, she couldn't speak. But from the whispered ooohs and ahhs from those around them, Symone knew she couldn't keep Josiah on his knees forever. "Yes. Yes!"

Josiah stood up, picked up Symone and swung her around as they kissed. The crowd acknowledged their union with a round of applause.

Twenty-one

The wedding ceremony was held in one of New Orleans' most visited and celebrated Bed and Breakfasts. It was the Oak Alley Inn, which had once been the refuge for hundreds of runaway slaves. Now it was owned by a distant relative of a free slave. Beneath a two-hundred-year-old live oak tree, overlooking a shimmering pond, Symone and Josiah exchanged wedding vows.

In attendance were about fifty friends and guests, mainly the New Orleans police force. Symone's best friend, Toni, and Josiah's family—his father, mother and sisters—had flown in to be a part of the blessed event. Toni was Symone's maid of honor; Josiah's father was the best man. With a special request from Symone, Omar had the honor of giving her away.

Symone was stunning. As a gift, Lieutenant Spaulding had bought Symone's wedding dress. She wore an original off-the-shoulder Vera Wang gown. It was of white lace and pearls, with a matching veil.

The minister stood before the guests and informed them that the bride and groom had prepared their own wedding vows. Symone was to recite her vows to Josiah first. She turned and handed Toni her bouquet of white lilies and baby's breath. She turned back to Josiah with a warm smile and teary eyes and took him by the hands.

"Josiah. Before I met you, I was walking in darkness. Light was absent from my eyes, my heart and my life. But you've managed to change all that with just a single touch.

You've given back to me joy, happiness and, most of all, love. And because of you I am no longer the same. In you I've found a friend, a lover and a protector. So today, in front of everyone here, I ask you to be my husband. I love you now and plan to love you as long as my life exists." Symone took the ring from Omar and slipped it on Josiah's hand.

Now it was Josiah's turn to recite his vows. For a moment, he stood silently. He gazed into Symone's beautiful eyes and a tear rolled down his cheek. He took her by the hands, turned them over and kissed her palms.

"Symone, I love you. I've never been to heaven, but God has entrusted me with an angel."

Symone cried beneath her veil. This day had been a long time coming for her and she didn't want it to end. She had found the man of her dreams.

Josiah continued his vows to her. "From the first moment I saw you and kissed your lips, there wasn't a doubt in my mind that I would make you my wife. When I experienced the darkest point of my life, you were the light that gave me hope and I was no longer afraid. And when my life was threatened, you rescued me." Tears streamed down his face. "And for that I give you my life, and my love, forever and ever, for as long as you would have me."

Josiah turned to his father, took Symone's ring and placed it on her finger. The couple then turned to the minister, who sealed their union with the traditional, "And now, by the power invested in me, I now pronounce you man and wife. Son, you may kiss your bride."

Josiah raised the veil from Symone's face and kissed her.

"Ladies and gentlemen," the minister said. "It is my pleasure to introduce to you Mr. and Mrs. Josiah La'Mon."

The guests applauded joyfully as a dozen white doves were released and flew cooing over their heads.

℃ 🌑 🌒

The reception had been catered by the inn, free of charge, and the music was provided by one of the city's well-known DJs. Toni happily embraced Symone and Josiah. "Congratulations, you two."

"Thank you, girl," Symone said, hugging Toni back.

"Josiah, you've made me the happiest woman on earth," Toni said, crying tears of joy.

Symone looked at her in surprise. "I thought I was the happiest woman here," she said, smiling.

"And you are. I'm happy because my best friend married a handsome man who, I know, must have other handsome friends that he can introduce me to."

The three shared a laugh.

"I thought you'd be upset that I'm taking your best friend away from you," Josiah said to Toni.

"No way. Symone and I will always be best friends, no matter what. Isn't that right, Symone?"

Symone kissed her on the cheek and said, "Friends forever."

"Be good to her, Josiah. She's a special lady, who deserves a good man."

"Don't worry, Toni. She has a good man, and I'll have no problem proving that."

Toni gave him a long look, then nodded her head. "I believe you."

℃ 🌑 🌒

The light of the setting sun reflected off the calm water. The serene view held Symone spellbound. Feeling blessed and overwhelmed with love, she stood on the bank alone, looking out in deep thought. She continually turned Jordan's class ring around her finger.

Omar walked up beside her. "Hey. What are doing over here? You're supposed to be celebrating with your new husband."

Symone turned to him, tears streaming down her face. "I never thought I could be so happy. I finally got everything I ever wanted. But not to have shared it with—"

Omar held her in his arms. "Ssh. Believe me, you're sharing it with him right now. Look around you, Symone. You have people who love you and share in your happiness. That's what Jordan would have wanted for you. And wherever he is, I'm sure he's smiling down on you right now. He wants you to enjoy your new life and not dwell on the past. I'm sure he would want you to release him and let him go."

Symone looked at Omar with warmth. She smiled and kissed him gently on the cheek. "Thank you." She was grateful to have a friend like Omar in her life. She knew she could always count on him to tell her exactly what she needed to hear.

"Now get back there and proudly stand beside your husband." Omar held out his arm. Symone wrapped her arm around it and allowed him to escort her back to the celebration, where Josiah's parents officially welcomed Symone into the family.

For the rest of the evening and well into the night, Symone and Josiah were showered with gifts, monetary as well as returnable. When it was time to leave, Toni, Omar, and Spaulding took rooms at the famous Bourbon Street

Hotel, while Symone, Josiah, and his family stayed at the Bed and Breakfast.

Under the illuminating light of the full moon and the low serenade of crickets and other night creatures, Symone and Josiah sat nestled in a wooden swing under a tree.

"You know, we haven't even discussed where we're gonna go on our honeymoon," she said, cuddled in his arms.

"Where do you want to go, baby?" Josiah kissed her on her head. "To the moon?"

Symone smiled contentedly. She was basking in the glory of his love. "I don't care. I'd go just about anywhere with you."

Josiah grinned as he held her closer. "How does it feel being a married woman now?"

"Like I'm finally complete. How about you? How does it feel being a married man?"

"Mmm...It feels like I'm stronger now. More aware of my purpose as a man and a husband. I mean, it's like I have something worth cherishing, worth protecting." He looked at Symone, resting in his arms. "And I owe it all to you."

Symone gazed into his loving eyes. "I don't know what to say after that, Josiah. That was really beautiful."

"But it's the truth. I've never felt this way about anyone before. It's a first for me, too."

Symone raised herself up and kissed his lips. "And that's how I want to make you feel every day. I want to be able to give you everything you ever hoped for in a wife."

"And, baby, you will. And I want to give you all the things my father has given my mother."

"And what's that, Josiah?"

"Love and happiness for the rest of our lives."

Under the moonlight, they embraced in a long, passionate kiss.

Twenty-two

Early the next morning, the newlyweds escorted their family and friends to the airport. Josiah and Symone saw off his family first. Then it was time for Symone to see Toni, Omar and Lieutenant Spaulding to their departure gate. Chattering away, Symone and Toni walked behind the men.

"So where are you two going to spend your honeymoon?" Toni asked, strolling arm and arm with Symone.

"We discussed it, but we haven't come to a decision on any place in particular. I think he wants to surprise me."

"How romantic. I gotta say, you sure did pick one helluva man. He's perfect for you, Symone. He's kind, considerate and handsome."

"Girl, I know." The two giggled like schoolgirls.

"I hope one day I can be so lucky."

"Toni, you will. And when you are, don't forget to invite me to the wedding."

"Humph. If we even get to that point, you'll have to remind me, because I will be in shock." The two laughed.

"But, seriously," Symone said. "Wherever he takes me, I'll be sure to call you with all the details."

"You better." Toni said, leaning into Symone's shoulder.

"Ssh. Listen." Symone said, eavesdropping on Josiah, Omar and Spaulding's conversation.

"So, Josiah. What are you going to do, now that you're not returning to the Bureau?" said the lieutenant.

Josiah placed his hand on Spaulding's shoulder. "Well, Lieutenant, I was thinking about deep-sea fishing."

Omar jerked his head in surprise. "You're gonna do what?"

Josiah smiled teasingly. "I'm kidding, you guys. But I'm not sure what my plans are, right now. I do know that I'm taking a break from the agency until Symone and I can settle down."

"I hear that. You two are just starting over, more or less..."

"Yeah. All my attention will be on making her happy. Whatever decision I do make about work, I want us to make it together."

Patting him on the back, Spaulding said, "You're a good man, Josiah."

"Thanks, Lieutenant."

"That goes for me too, man," Omar said, shaking Josiah's hand.

"Thanks. That means a lot, coming from the two of you. I promise to take good care of her," Josiah said.

Omar gave him a quick glance. "Oh, we're not worried about that. But do me a favor."

"Sure. What?"

Omar leaned into Josiah and spoke low. "Make sure she doesn't boss you around. She can get pretty good at that, take if from me."

Josiah chuckled. "Sure. But you know Symone. She can be headstrong when she wants to be."

Spaulding placed his hand on Josiah's shoulder. "That's when you give her something to do, like having babies."

Symone and Toni snickered secretly at the men's conversation.

Before they left, Symone took the opportunity to thank Spaulding again. "Lieutenant. I wanted to say thank you for everything you've done for me. And I'm not just talking about making my wedding day one to remember, but for everything you've done for me in the past."

"You don't have to thank me, Symone."

"Yeah, I do. That's why this is not going to be easy for me to do. But here goes." Symone pulled from her pocket her shield and badge. "I never thought the day would come that I would be doing this."

"Symone."

"I know what you're going to say, Lieutenant, but hear me out. All my life I have come to the rescue of others, always there in the nick of time. I patterned my life around saving people, a decree I've lived by for thirteen years. And now, I have someone who wants to rescue me. Frankly, I'm looking forward to it." Symone looked in Josiah's direction. "He's the best thing that my life has ever had." She turned back to the lieutenant. "So that's why, as of now, I am resigning my position as a police officer." Symone placed her badge in his palm and closed his hand over it.

Spaulding didn't object. He just looked at her with admiration and sorrow. "I'm not going to say I'm not disappointed, but I will honor your request. You're going to be hard to replace, Detective."

Symone held back the tears. "No, I won't. There's always someone to take my place."

"Not like you. You're one of a kind. Does Omar know?"

"Mmm. He has an idea."

"So what are you going to do with yourself?"

"I was thinking about kids. I want to have a lot of them."

Spaulding laughed. "Well, you'll definitely have plenty of time," he said with a grin. "In that case, I guess this is our final good-bye."

"It's never good-bye, Lieutenant. Just so long, for now." Symone hugged him, then escorted him over to the others.

Symone and Josiah walked them to the departure gate as their flight was announced over the P.A. system.

Symone stood at the entrance to the gate. "Omar, do me a favor," she said. "Keep an eye on Toni for me. You know, invite her over for dinner every now and again."

"Sure." He hugged her for the last time. "And don't worry about us. You just enjoy being a wife to that guy."

"I will. And tell Monica I said have a healthy, beautiful baby. For me."

"We will. Stay in touch," he said finally.

When the threesome was safely aboard the plane, Symone and Josiah stood at the airport window. The plane went down the runway and took to the sky. They watched until it ascended out of sight.

Josiah watched a lone tear roll down Symone's face. He gently wiped it away with his finger. "Are those tears of regret?"

Smiling, she said, "Tears of joy."

He caressed her cheek. "I guess this is it. Everybody's gone and it's just me and you."

Symone smiled at him. "Finally."

They left the departure gate and headed to the airport garage and their car.

"You know what? I got a great idea," he said, wrapping his arm around her waist.

Laying her head on his shoulder, she said, "What?"

"When we get back to the hotel, let's pack our things and take a trip."

They exited the elevator and got to their car; then Symone stopped abruptly.

"What's the matter, you forgot something?" asked Josiah.

"No. It just dawned on me that this is how it all began." She leaned into the car and seductively pulled Josiah against her body. She batted her eyelashes flirtatiously, then kissed him.

"If you keep that up," he said, looking at her with passion in his eyes, "I'm going to start something."

"Don't you remember? This is how we met. You came to pick me up at the airport."

Josiah grinned. "Oh, yeah. That day seems like it happened a long time ago."

"But do you remember the first words you said to me?"

"Yeah. I kind of said something like this." He leaned forward and kissed her deeply.

Epilogue

On the shores of the Cayman Islands, where the pink, sandy beaches met the crystal-blue water, and enchanted breezes whispered lullabies through the palm trees was where Symone and Josiah spent three glorious weeks on their honeymoon. Exotic birds soared in the sky, while below, the sweet sounds of steel drums and sassy horns serenaded the happy couple day and night at their romantic island hideaway.

They spent their days skinny-dipping in a private lagoon, miles from the crowded hotel, and their nights making love beneath the blue-black sky.

Under the shade of two palm trees, Symone and Josiah swung lazily together in a large hammock. The sun shone brightly, but the breeze off the water was mild. Symone lay on top of Josiah, wearing nothing more than her bikini bottom.

"Oh, I wish we could stay here forever. But we only have one more day to spend in paradise," she said, inhaling the sweet-smelling air.

"If you don't want to leave, we don't have to."

Symone chuckled. "Oh, sure. We can pitch a tent and live like beach bums."

"No, I'm serious," Josiah said.

Symone raised herself up and looked him in the face. "And I'm serious too, Josiah. We can't afford to live like this. Although we're not broke, we have to be more sensible with the money we do have."

"But this is not a joke, baby. This place, these trees, that bungalow we've been staying in, it's ours."

Symone stared at him in bewilderment. "I don't understand what you're trying to say. Are you saying that we can live here for free, no strings attached, nobody to come and tell us to leave?"

"That's exactly what I'm saying."

Symone began pinching his side. "Don't play with me, man. If this is a joke, you better tell me right now."

"Ouch! I'm serious. It's not a joke. I can prove it."

"How?"

"I have the deed in a safe-deposit box at the bank in town."

"But how?"

"It was a wedding gift from my parents, along with some savings bonds that will definitely come in handy. This place was where they spent their honeymoon thirty-five years ago. They liked it so much, they bought it."

Symone jumped up hysterically, kissed and hugged Josiah. "I can't believe it! I can't believe it! You kept this from me all this time?"

"Because I wanted to surprise you. Now, aren't you surprised?"

"Heck, yeah. I mean, look at this place. It's beautiful. Anybody would be crazy if they didn't want to stay here for the rest of their lives. And we are talking permanent, aren't we?"

"Yes. I plan to raise our children here. We'll be like Adam and Eve in the garden of Eden."

Symone snuggled against his chest. "And, speaking of children, I got something to tell you."

Josiah looked at her suspiciously. "Are you telling me—"

"Yes. I think so."

"Oh my God. Are you telling me I'm going to be a father?"

"I'm saying it's a possibility. But don't quote me on it. It's almost too soon to tell.. And I still have to see a doctor."

"When? As soon as we get back home?"

"But we are home, baby," she said with a giggle.

"Oh, yeah."

And so the Cayman Islands became Symone and Josiah's permanent home, where they raised their children. Symone had twins, a girl and a boy—Jordan and Jennell.

Josiah opened up a private security company on the island. He had a team of trained men, who protected the stores and businesses throughout the island and beyond. Symone stayed at home and raised their children.

Every year during the holidays, they would travel back to Maryland and New Orleans to visit friends and loved ones. But the island was what they called home. A paradise where they lived out the rest of their lives together.

Charlene Berry was born in Maryland and currently lives in Irvington, New Jersey, where she works as an administrative assistant.

Charlene is the author of *Love's Deceptions*, one of Genesis' first Indigo titles. For her second Indigo romance, *Cajun Heat,* she spent time with the police force, culling through public records on serial killers, to give authenticity to that aspect of her story.

INDIGO: Sensuous Love Stories *Order Form*

Mail to:
Genesis Press, Inc.
315 3rd Avenue North
Columbus, MS 39701

Visit our website at

http://www.genesis-press.com

Name ————————————————————

Address ————————————————————

City/State/Zip ————————————————

1999 INDIGO TITLES

Qty	Title	Author	Price	Total
	Somebody's Someone	Sinclair LeBeau	$8.95	
	Interlude	Donna Hill	$8.95	
	The Price of Love	Beverly Clark	$8.95	
	Unconditional Love	Alicia Wiggins	$8.95	
	Mae's Promise	Melody Walcott	$8.95	
	Whispers in the Night	Dorothy Love	$8.95	
	No Regrets (paperback reprint)	Mildred Riley	$8.95	
	Kiss or Keep	D.Y. Phillips	$8.95	
	Naked Soul (paperback reprint)	Gwynne Forster	$8.95	
	Pride and Joi (paperback Reprint)	Gay G. Gunn	$8.95	
	A Love to Cherish (paperback reprint)	Beverly Clark	$8.95	
	Caught in a Trap	Andree Jackson	$8.95	
	Truly Inseparable (paperback reprint)	Wanda Thomas	$8.95	
	A Lighter Shade of Brown	Vicki Andrews	$8.95	
	Cajun Heat	Charlene Berry	$8.95	

**Use this order form
or call:
1-888-INDIGO1**
(1-888-463-4461)

TOTAL ————

Shipping & Handling ————
($3.00 first book $1.00 each additional book)

TOTAL Amount Enclosed ————

MS Residents add 7% sales tax